Shelley no longer expected to find a Prince Charming

Rather she hoped to find someone with whom she could, through determined effort and lots of compromise, live in reasonable harmony for the rest of her life and his. She had long since lost faith in the elusive, mythical, magical zing, the instantaneous awareness of sexual chemistry when she looked in a man's eyes, the breathless anticipation of a touch, the heart-stopping thrill when that touch finally came.

And then Garrick Booth kissed her.

Dear Reader,

What is more appealing, more enduring, than *Cinderella, Beauty and the Beast* and *Pygmalion*? Fairy tales and legends are basic human stories, retold in every age, in their own way. Romance stories, at heart, are the happily ever after of every story we listened to as children.

That was the inspiration for our 1993 yearlong Lovers & Legends miniseries. One book each month is a fairy tale retold in sizzling Temptation-style!

April brings Glenda Sanders's *Dr. Hunk,* a tender yet comical modern-day version of *The Frog Prince.* Heroine Shelley Peters discovers her Prince in the most unlikely man—Dr. Garrick Booth, who has devoted most of his energies to researching the mating habits of insects! We're also pleased to congratulate Glenda on being the Rita Award Winner for the Best Short Contemporary Series Romance, 1991 for her Temptation novel *A Human Touch.*

In the coming months, we have stories from popular authors including Kelly Street, *The Virgin and the Unicorn* (unicorn myths), Gina Wilkins, *When It's Right* (*The Princess and the Pea*) and Lynn Michaels, *Second Sight* (*The Ugly Duckling*).

We hope you enjoy the magic of Lovers & Legends, plus all the other terrific Temptation novels coming in 1993!

Birgit Davis-Todd
Senior Editor

P.S. We love to hear from our readers.

Dr. Hunk

Glenda Sanders

Harlequin Books

TORONTO • NEW YORK • LONDON
AMSTERDAM • PARIS • SYDNEY • HAMBURG
STOCKHOLM • ATHENS • TOKYO • MILAN
MADRID • WARSAW • BUDAPEST • AUCKLAND

I wish to extend my thanks to Dr. E.
(for entomologist!) for opening my eyes
to the mating behavior of those naughty moths;
to his lovely wife, for her insight
into an entomologist's private view of the world;
and to Brenda S., who allowed me to watch her
sort mail and trail her on her delivery route.
Your generosity of time and knowledge
contributed to the richness of this story.

Published April 1993

ISBN 0-373-25537-3

DR. HUNK

Printed in U.S.A.

Prologue

"IT'S WORSE THAN I thought."

"Hmm?" Dr. Garrick Booth looked up from the honey-water solution he was mixing at a stainless steel utility sink. "What's worse than you thought?"

"You," his sister Kelsey said dramatically, making a sweeping motion with her arm that took in the windows with their spartan, sagging bamboo roll-up shades, the makeshift board-and-concrete-block shelves, and the two work islands—one of stainless steel that adjoined the sink, the other of easy-care laminate over which were strewn his microscope, loupes, timers and notebooks. "This place. The way you live. I suspected as much from what Mother said after her visit."

Gere grimaced, then pushed his patched, ill-fitting glasses back into place and stared intently at his sister. Eyes the same golden green as his own stared back at him, and Kelsey's jaw was thrust outward and upward. Gere steeled himself for the concerned-parent lecture he knew was imminent. When Kelsey got on one of her wild tangents, she wasn't easily diverted.

"Mother loved my place," he said matter-of-factly. "She was green with envy."

"Oh, yes. Indeed, she was. After all, you never have to *leave* for anything. She has to get dressed and drive to the university to do her work. Sometimes she even has to—" She gave an exaggerated gasp and feigned a shudder of horror. "*Interact* with people."

"Are you trying to make a point?"

"No one pulls the wool over your eyes for long, do they? The point, Big Brother, is that you are a total recluse here. You're totally cut off from civilization."

Gere capped the plastic jug of honey and water and shook it. "That's patently absurd. I subscribe to a newspaper, two newsmagazines and half a dozen scientific journals. *And* I watch the news every night."

Kelsey sniffed disdainfully. "Well, give the man a banana! He knows all about earthquakes that hit the far side of the earth, and who's running for Congress."

"What would I want with a banana?" Gere mumbled.

Kelsey continued undeterred. "I'll bet you'd be on the cutting edge of knowledge if they identified a strain of mutated lepidoptera in the foothills of the Tibetan mountains."

"What would I want with a banana?" Gere repeated.

Kelsey sighed. "Oh, Gere. That's exactly what I mean. It's just an expression, and not even a particularly new one. When was the last time you *talked* to someone?"

"Mrs. Northbrook is here every Thursday. We always talk."

"Mrs. Northbrook?"

"She cleans the house and does the grocery shopping."

"How old is this Mrs. Northbrook?"

"Old? I don't know. I've never asked."

"What's even worse, you probably didn't even notice."

"Of course, I noticed. She's... Well, she's not young, but she's not elderly. She's ... somewhere in between."

"Somewhere?" Kelsey echoed.

"It's not polite to ask a woman's age."

"And what do you and Mrs. Northbrook talk about?"

Garrick shrugged. "Groceries, and whether or not the floors need waxing, or just wet mopping."

"How scintillating."

"Why don't you join us Thursday. We'll serve tea and crumpets and have a party."

"Go ahead. Take that smug, superior tone. You know why they don't send mules to college."

"Mules to college?"

Kelsey rolled her eyes in exasperation. "You're hopeless, Gere. That one's as old as Methuselah, and you've never even heard it! They don't send mules to college because no one likes a smartass."

"Is there a point you're trying to make?"

"No one with two Ph.D.'s—not even a bona fide smartass—could be as oblivious to what I'm trying to point out as you pretend to be."

"I *am* oblivious. What's your point?"

He instantly regretted having asked. Although she was four years younger than he, Kelsey had always tended to mother him. Whether it was simply her nature to do so, or whether it was a survival trait developed to compensate for their lack of conventional mothering Gere didn't know. He watched her square her shoulders, cross her arms over her waist and assume a posture of long-suffering patience.

"This isn't a healthy situation, Gere. You never go anywhere."

"I don't need to. I've got everything I need right here, and when I do need something, I put it on the list for Mrs. Northbrook."

"You don't have a life outside of your work! You have no social life. You don't talk to anyone your own age. When was the last time you had a date?" She didn't give him time to reply before pressing on. "For that matter, when was the last time you *saw* a woman, let alone kissed one?"

"You're meddling," Gere said.

"I'm your sister. It gives me a license. You can't go on like this, Gere. You're beginning to make Howard Hughes look like an extrovert."

"You're nagging, too."

"I'm your sister. It gives me a license."

"If I get an inflamed appendix, I hope you don't think that being my sister gives you a license to perform an appendectomy!"

"See? You're already turning into a cynic. One of these days you're going to open your mouth to talk and realize that your vocal chords have shriveled up from lack of use."

"Now you *are* being ridiculous! I talk to the dogs every day."

"And I suppose they lick you behind the ears and keep you warm at night?"

"Don't be vulgar, Kelsey."

"I'm trying to shock you into seeing how…unnatural this situation is. You're going to be thirty next week, not ninety. You're a healthy man. You must think about women. Don't you ever get lonely?"

Gere set his jaw and crossed the room to pour the honey water into the sponges resting atop the net covering several small plastic cages. Inside the plastic cages were moths.

"I'm too busy to be lonely," he said.

"Everybody gets lonely sometimes," Kelsey said.

Gere frowned. "Well, if and when I ever get lonely, I'll do something about it."

Kelsey waited a moment before saying, gently, "I knew you were going to get hurt. You're so tunnel-visioned that you couldn't see it coming."

"See what?" Gere countered, feigning ignorance.

"That you and the institute were just an interesting interlude to Dr. Sondra Updike, while you thought—"

"Go ahead," Gere said, when she hesitated. "Don't turn shy now. Tell me what I thought."

"You know as well as I do that you thought you and the beautiful doctor were a team, dedicated to science and to each other for life. Just like our parents."

"So?" Gere said. "It didn't work out that way."

"That witch hogged the credit for the work the two of you did together and used it as a springboard for a great teaching position," Kelsey reminded. "That had to hurt, Gere. Why can't you admit it?"

"It's history," Gere replied, his cheeks growing hot with the emotion he was holding in check. "She wanted glory and a prestigious teaching job. I wanted to stay here and work. She left, and I stayed. I lived through it."

Kelsey's eyes flashed in challenge. "Did you?"

"Stick a mirror under my nose. I'm breathing."

"Oh, you're breathing. And you're working. But you're not doing much living."

Gere's thunderous scowl quelled further argument. Kelsey's features softened in concern. "You bought into the myth, Gere," she said gently. "Don't let it destroy you, too."

Gere gave Kelsey a long, hard stare. "Are you on medication of some kind?"

"Don't pull that flippant garbage on me."

"I don't know what you're talking about."

"I'm talking about our parents. They were the perfect team. Love and science. Unity of purpose. Until Father died, and Mother buried herself in her work."

"She's doing valuable research work."

"Mmm-hmm. But she has no life outside of research. She cut herself off from anything or anyone who required emotional energy—including her own children."

"We were always cared for."

"By hired hands," Kelsey said. "But that's not what we're discussing. We're discussing *you*. There's still time to save you, and I don't intend to stand by in silence while you pattern your life after hers and self-destruct."

"I can believe the not-standing-by-in-silence part," Gere retorted.

Their gazes locked for a moment in mutual challenge.

"You're burying yourself alive," she warned.

"Look, Kelsey, you like being surrounded by people. You like being on teams, so you played every sport they'd let girls play. You like bossing people around, so you got a teacher's certificate and became a coach. That way, you're surrounded by students who have to do what you tell them to do."

"We're not discussing me," she said.

"I was merely pointing out the contrasts in our lifestyles and attendant needs. You're a high school coach because being a high school coach fulfills your needs—"

"Perfectly," Kelsey interjected.

"Obviously," Gere said dryly. He'd noticed it throughout her visit. A quiet confidence and contentment showed in her every move, as much a part of her fit golden-girl looks as the sun streaks shooting through her light brown hair or the healthy glow of her slightly olive skin. "And the institute suits my needs. I don't need a lot of people around. I don't need the noise, or the pressure. I don't want to have to explain or apologize when I get too involved in my work to make polite conversation."

"No one expects you to become a social butterfly." She giggled. "I wasn't even trying to be funny."

"You weren't succeeding."

Kelsey gave him an exasperated scowl. "You above anyone else should appreciate entomological humor. A social butterfly—!"

She appeared so inordinately pleased with the accidental pun that Gere allowed himself a sliver of hope that she might become sidetracked from her lecture. But apparently, after two years of outfoxing students set on sidetracking any lecture coming their way, she had developed the ability to bounce back to a topic at the precise point from which she'd been diverted.

"You may not need people around you when you work, but you're a human being. You need some human companionship, some socialization."

Gere harrumphed his disdain for the idea. His attitude only incited Kelsey. "Look at you, Gere," she said, raising her hand in a dramatic gesture. "You're a good-looking man. When was the last time you had a decent haircut?"

"It hasn't been— I just trimmed it a little when it began to get—"

"How long do you intend to wear a pair of glasses held together with a glob of strapping tape?"

Gere unconsciously raised his hand to push the glasses higher on the bridge of his nose. "This is my old spare. My good pair got broken, and the prescription was too old for the optician to make new lenses. I have an appointment next week for an exam— Oh, hell!"

"Next week, or this week?" Kelsey asked.

"Last week," Gere admitted with a dismal sigh.

Kelsey's sigh was equally dismal. "Oh, Gere."

"I'll make another appointment. These aren't exactly comfortable, you know."

"When was the last time you bought yourself a shirt?"

Gere looked down at the Harvard seal covering his chest. "A shirt? This is the last shirt I have left from undergraduate days."

"Really? Why, it's probably not more than eight or nine years old."

"It's clean. And it's soft."

"It has no sleeves."

"I cut them out. They were too hot for Florida. Now it's perfect."

"And those shorts?"

"Used to be my favorite jeans. Then the knees wore out, so I cut them off. They're perfect, too."

"At least the shoes are good. Loafers without socks are good."

"No clean socks," Gere explained. "Which reminds me—my birthday's coming up. Why don't you give me some socks so I have enough to make it a week between laundries?"

He didn't like the smile that slid onto Kelsey's face. It was sly. And, unless he was mistaken, slightly sadistic. It made him extremely uneasy.

"Oh, I've already got something in mind for your birthday, Big Brother," she said. "Something far better for you, and far more interesting than socks."

Gere told himself that the feeling of dread in his gut was unwarranted. After all, Kelsey was only going to be in Florida for a few days. By his birthday she'd be in Indiana, with the new school year well under way. She couldn't do anything too drastic from over a thousand miles away, could she?

The rationalization was not reassuring. All in all, he'd have felt a lot better if she'd asked what color socks he wanted.

1

MAIL CARRIER SHELLEY Peters wrinkled her nose and paused to take a second look at the letter she was about to put into one of several hundred narrow vertical slots on the sorting rack in front of her. Each of the vertical slots represented a stop on a route of over 450, and each of the thousands of envelopes in the canvas hamper to her right belonged in a specific slot on the rack that spanned from waist height to above her head.

Although elegant, the peach-colored, textured stationery would not have attracted her attention, but the letter was saturated with enough expensive perfume to make a horse snort. Shelley looked closely at the address written in brown ink in a large, feminine scroll. Practice had given her the ability to look at addresses and see only the street name and number—enough information to get the mail into the proper slot for loading. This time, though, she noticed the name, as well. She chuckled. *Dr. Hunk?*

The street in the address was toward the end of her route, and there were only four stops along that road. Curiosity thoroughly piqued, she pulled the envelopes already in the slot for that street number and skimmed them. Unless she was mistaken, that number belonged to...yes. She was right. It was that research place with the fancy name, the one with the fenced yard and the two Dalmatians that barked hysterically at her four-wheel drive Jeep when she pulled up to the roadside mailbox. There was a doctor of some kind who got lots of scientific magazines. She couldn't recall his name, but she was certain it wasn't Hunk—Hunk she would have remembered.

Booth. That was it. Dr. Garrick Booth—plainly spelled out on the phone bill for the Institute for Entomologic and Chemical Research. Shelley shook her head. Talk about a mouthful name! What was entomologic research, anyway? The term *entomology* was vaguely familiar, but she was ten years removed from high school science.

Funny, Shelley thought, the preconceived notions people formed. She'd always imagined the unseen doctor as an aging, bookish man, probably absent-minded. Apparently someone from Kansas with pretty handwriting, expensive perfume and lots of chutzpah had a different vision of the mysterious scientist.

With a shrug of dismissal, Shelley shoved the Dr. Hunk letter into the sorting slot along with the rest of the mail for the institute, involuntarily wrinkling her nose again as the strong scent wafted out.

Once the letters were sorted, she pulled them from the rack in delivery-route order and transferred them to long trays that would be loaded onto her Jeep along with the parcels, the certified and insured mail—which required the signature of the recipient—and the flats, or oversize envelopes and magazines. She smelled the Dr. Hunk letter again when she loaded the mail into the tray, and yet again when she lifted the tray from the loading cart to put it in the cargo space of the Jeep. After that, she promptly forgot about it as she focused on maneuvering the Jeep through the midmorning traffic in downtown Tropical City on the way to her delivery route.

There was not a great deal of traffic to maneuver through. Compared to nearby Orlando or the teeming suburbs in neighboring Seminole County where Shelley had grown up, the motor vehicle activity in Tropical City barely qualified as "traffic." Tropical City was still a lazy little burg, one of the last rural refuges defiantly fending off Orlando's urban sprawl. In addition to the post office, the downtown consisted of two banks, a dime store, three clothing stores, the city hall, the police station and two cafés, all of which Shelley passed on the way to the first half of her route, which took in a small subdivision about a mile north of downtown.

Once she left the subdivision, her route was mostly in rural areas, down winding country roads where the houses were half a mile apart. By early afternoon the apricot "Dr. Hunk" letter had worked its way close enough to the top of the mail stack for the perfume to become cloying in the midday heat. It was going to be a relief to stuff it in the doctor's mailbox so she wouldn't have to smell it anymore.

As usual, the Dalmatians loped across the vast front lawn, barking hysterically, when she stopped the Jeep next to the mailbox. Glad they were on the other side of the fence, Shelley nevertheless spoke to them as she gathered the doctor's mail, wanting them to be accustomed to the sound of her voice in case they ever decided to take a flying leap over that fence. "Hey, boys. Hi, ya. How are you doing today? Guarding the institute, eh?"

They quieted and sat down, watching her as she stuffed the doctor's phone bill, the apricot letter and the latest issue of *Science* magazine into the mailbox and pushed it shut. "Somebody talks to you guys, don't they? You're friendly, aren't you? All that barking's just a big act."

As she spoke, she scrutinized the sprawling grounds of the Institute for Entomologic and Chemical Research. She didn't know whether the mysterious Dr. Booth was a hunk, but the institute he ran was quite impressive. The fence enclosed at least an acre, and the wooded area abutting the tree-studded lawns stretched at least another five. The garage was a good hundred and fifty feet from the wrought-iron security gate that opened onto the driveway. Centered on the lawn was a rambling brick building that looked more like a house than a scientific think tank.

Did the doctor live there, Shelley wondered, or merely work there? She tried to recall whether most of his mail was strictly professional, or whether he received personal correspondence, as well. Aside from the imposing name of the institute and the sometimes-freakish scientific publications, she'd never paid much attention to the mail she delivered to this particular box.

Of course, she thought as she pulled the Jeep back onto the road, the apricot-colored letter had changed that. She'd be paying attention in the future—at least until she got a good look at the elusive Dr. Hunk!

Beyond the institute, her route was comprised of several isolated houses, a filling station, a church, an automobile junkyard and a convenience store. Her last stop was a small mobile home park with a dozen communal boxes, each of which held mail slots for ten individual lots. In the winter, the park was filled with snowbirds and retirees fleeing the Northern winters. This time of year, it was only about half full, which meant she finished quickly.

As a contract carrier, she was paid according to a formula based on the number of stops on her delivery route, rather than on the hours she worked. So, like many of her peers, Shelley seldom took time for an official meal break, preferring instead to grab a quick snack somewhere along the way to finish earlier in the afternoon. Over the long, hot Florida summer, she had developed the habit of stopping at the convenience store to have a soda and cool off in the store's air-conditioned interior when she carried in the day's mail.

Today was no different. Smiling, Shelley handed the slim bundle of envelopes to the counter clerk, Paula. The thirtyish, slightly plump clerk smiled back and said, "All good news today, I hope."

Familiar with the clichéd quip and all its variations, Shelley joked back, "I think I saw one from Mel Gibson marked 'Personal.'"

"From your lips to Mel-my-baby's ears," Paula said, casting a lusty glance at the *Lethal Weapon 3* poster on the wall behind the counter.

Shelley walked to the self-serve soda fountain at the back of the store and pumped herself a diet soda, then brought it to the counter to pay for it.

"Still hot out there?" Paula asked.

"Not quite as bad as last week," Shelley replied. "There's a touch of fall in the air."

"Must be," Paula said. "My dad's allergies have been acting up. He calls it the Fall Curse. He's been sneezing his way through late September for as long as I can remember."

"You grew up in Tropical City, didn't you?" Shelley asked.

"Yep. I'm one of that endangered species—a native Floridian."

"What do you know about that research place on Palmetto Road?" Shelley inquired, grasping the opportunity to fish for information while the store wasn't crowded.

"Research place?"

"The Institute for Entomologic and Chemical Research."

"Oh!" Paula exclaimed, as though a light bulb had just turned on above her curly, too-yellow locks. "You mean the Hoffmann place. Some weirdo doctor bought it after the Hoffmanns' divorce. What a mess. They say he came home early from a business trip and she was entertaining in the master suite, so to speak. It was nasty."

"Weirdo?" Shelley prompted, to get Paula back on track.

"The bug man. Anyone who studies bugs for a living has got to be weird."

Bugs, Shelley thought. *So that's what entomology is.*

"They wrote a story about him in the paper once," Paula said. "He's some kind of genius."

"How old is he?"

Paula shrugged. "Who knows? No one around here's ever seen him. Most people call him 'the mad scientist.' He must be rich, though."

"Rich?"

"That house, with all that land? He probably paid half a million dollars for it."

So we have a rich, weird genius who gets mail addressed to Dr. Hunk. It was something to think about when she was out on her route—especially since the Dr. Hunk letters kept coming.

In different envelopes.

With different scents.
From different parts of the country.

"GERE. WHAT A PLEASANT surprise."

The sarcasm in Kelsey's voice raised Gere's ire to an even higher level of irritation. If she hadn't anticipated he'd call her, she was an idiot! "Don't you 'pleasant surprise' me!" he thundered into the telephone receiver. "You know why I'm calling."

"You must have found out about my present. Happy birthday."

"You're lucky you're half a continent away, or I might be tempted to resort to physical violence." She was lucky he hadn't chartered a plane so he could *throttle* her!

"Is that any way to talk to a devoted sister?"

"How dare you... *publish* my address in a ... a ... *rag?*"

Kelsey laughed. "Oh, Gere. Don't be melodramatic. It's one of the most respectable lonely hearts classifieds in the country."

"So you admit placing the ad."

"Admit it? Of course, I admit it. I told you I had something special lined up for your birthday."

" 'Expert on insect reproduction seeks human involvement and sensual stimulation. Send perfumed replies to Dr. Hunk.' "

"It's a masterpiece, isn't it?" Kelsey said proudly.

"It's a travesty," Gere retorted. "It's an invasion of my privacy! My address. My work. *You involved my work!* If anyone in my field reads it, I'll never live down the notoriety."

"Oh, posh! Those ads are like dark bars where married men take married women for an assignation. If anyone saw it and spread it around, they'd have to explain why and how they happened to see it."

"It'll get out. Just wait and see. There aren't that many entomologists, and I'm the *only* scientist in Tropical City. I'll be an object of ridicule."

"You'll be an object of awe and envy. You'll have panache. Charisma. Female lab assistants will cast off their lab coats and offer themselves to you, *Dr. Hunk*."

"Good grief, Kelsey. Grandmother would faint dead away if she heard you talk like that. I don't know where you get it."

"I'm a changeling, remember. The only one in the family who *isn't* a scientist. While the rest of you have been peering through microscopes, I've been out in the real world, living. I'm trying to introduce you to life, if you'd just cooperate. Hold on a minute, will you?"

Gere fumed as he heard her muffled, "Hey, can you guys turn that TV down just a bit? I'm on long distance." Then she explained, "The teachers' lounge is small, and the English teachers are watching a soap opera on television. You were saying?"

"My address, Kelsey! What if some woman shows up on my doorstep?"

"Bravo for her! Maybe she'll be beautiful. At the very least, she'll be a fellow human being."

"Who knows what kind of unbalanced . . . *perverts* answer those ads? Some woman could become obsessed like that woman in— What was that movie you rented when you were here?"

"*Fatal Attraction.* That's very unlikely, Gere. And if it does, you can take care of yourself. You're a healthy physical specimen. And besides, you have the dogs to protect you."

"I'm glad you find this amusing." *She was impossible! A lonely hearts ad. Of all the harebrained ideas!*

"I find it exciting," Kelsey said. "I wanted to shake up your well-ordered little existence, and it sounds as though I've succeeded. Why don't you read the letters and see if one of the writers appeals to you?"

"You have a peculiar sense of humor, Kelsey."

"Because I'm the first Booth in three generations to actually employ their sense of humor. I'm working on you, though. If I can get you a life, you might revive yours."

Gere's fingers contracted around the telephone receiver. "I have a fine sense of humor. Just the other day a colleague of mine sent me a remarkable joke about a nearsighted gypsy moth who—"

"Spare me moth jokes, or the one about the two compounds in the bottom of the centrifuge! Listen, my conference period's almost over, and I want to grab a bottle of water before my next class. And Gere—"

"Hmm?"

"I love hearing from you, but *please* don't call me at school again unless it's an emergency."

"It *was* an emergency."

"Whatever you say. Listen, I really have to go. The bell's about to ring, and I want to get to the gym before the little darlings get out of class and the hallways turn into New York subway terminals. Ta-ta, Big Brother. Enjoy your mail!"

Gere hung up the phone none too gently. *Enjoy his mail!* If word of that lonely hearts club ad got out, he was going to be the laughingstock of the entire scientific community.

No life! No sense of humor! he fumed. Kelsey was way over the line. She was three ants short of a picnic.

He had a perfectly nice life, with challenging, meaningful work. And he certainly had a sense of humor. Just thinking about the nearsighted gypsy moth made him laugh out loud.

Maybe Kelsey *was* a changeling. Immediately he shook his head, rejecting the superstition-based theory. No, he was a scientist, and scientists did not believe in superstitious claptrap.

SHELLEY PUSHED THE BELL again and waited, simmering with impatient frustration while the Dalmatians eyed her menacingly from the other side of the fence and the locked gate.

Thwarted! Just when she'd thought she was going to get a look at the elusive Dr. Hunk! She sighed as she settled back into the driver's seat of her Jeep, then ran a wet paper towel over her face and took a swig of water from her plastic sipper mug. Then she reached for her clipboard with the "Attempted Delivery" forms. Almost October, and it was pressing ninety again. And worse, Dr. Hunk remained a mystery man.

But not for long. After filling out the form and stuffing it into Dr. Hunk's mailbox, she took out her pad of sticky notes and wrote:

Attention: Clerk
Please take note of whoever claims this parcel and see me. I want details!

She underlined the last word a few times for emphasis and signed the note. Then, satisfied, she stuck it over the address of the registered letter she'd tried to deliver to the mysterious Dr. Booth. If she couldn't see him personally, at least she'd find out *something* about him.

She took another draft from the mug, then pulled back onto the road.

Gere reached the front of the house just in time to see the mail truck drive away. So he *had* heard the driveway bell. It wasn't always easy to tell from the lab. He ran through a list of mail he was expecting, and decided it was either a piece of equipment or the eyeglasses he'd special ordered.

The dogs nearly knocked him over as he stepped out of the house. Laughing, he shoved them down, petting each in turn. "Hey, Wigglesworth. Good boy. How's it shaking? And you, von Frisch— Is Wigglesworth treating you okay?"

The yellow package notice confirmed that the mailman had, indeed, probably rung the bell. He gave the matter little thought on the way to the house. Tomorrow was Thursday; he'd send Mrs. Northbrook to the post office with the yellow slip.

On Friday morning, Shelley heard a man call out her name just as she was reaching for the heavy door of the employees' entrance to the post office. She stopped and turned to see who it was. Stepping aside, out of the way of the door, which opened outward, she said, "George. Hi. What's up?"

George moved within easy conversational range and asked, "You wanted to know about that insured parcel for Booth?"

"He came in for it?" Shelley asked anxiously, glad it was George who'd handled the transaction. George was not only the most experienced counter clerk at the post office, he was the most efficient. He was also a genuinely nice person. "What'd he look like?" she pressed, knowing George would tell her.

"*He* was a *she*," George replied.

"A woman?" Shelley hadn't expected that. It hadn't occurred to her that Dr. Hunk could be married, or have a live-in lover. There was never any mail for a Mrs. Booth, never anything for anyone other than the doctor or the research institute. "Well, what did *she* look like?"

"I knew you were going to ask that," George said, deliberately stalling just to tease her.

"Gee-orge," Shelley pleaded.

"Oh, all right," George acquiesced. "I knew you'd want to know, so I made a point of checking her out. She had salt-and-pepper hair, and she was wearing a denim skirt, and sensible shoes. Exactly the way you'd expect a housekeeper to look."

"Housekeeper?"

"That's who she said she was—the doctor's housekeeper. She wanted to sign for the parcel, but it was restricted delivery so we couldn't let her have it."

"Did she say anything...interesting?"

"Interesting?"

"About the doctor."

"No. Just that he'd probably call to have the parcel put back on the truck because he wouldn't want to make the trip to the post office."

"Did she say... Is he...well, incapacitated or anything?"

"She didn't say." He gave her a questioning look. "You got something going with the doctor?"

Shelley frowned. "I don't have *anything* going with anyone right now. I haven't even *seen* the doctor. He's just been getting some interesting mail."

George's curiosity was piqued. "Interesting how?"

"Pastel, perfumed and ex-pensive."

George gave a whistle of appreciation.

"Addressed to Dr. Hunk," Shelley added dramatically.

"You're kidding!"

"I kid you not," Shelley said. "Ever since I got this route, it's been science magazines and official-looking stuff addressed to Dr. Garrick Booth or that research institute place. Then, pow! Perfumed letters to Dr. Hunk."

"Think the doctor got himself a girlfriend?"

"A girlfriend? He got himself a harem. The letters are coming in from all over."

"What'd he do—advertise?"

"It looks that way," Shelley said, and then added, with a thoughtful sigh, "Maybe he's lonely."

"Thinking of keeping him company?" George teased.

Shelley grinned. "I might...if he were good-looking enough."

"Tall, dark and handsome, of course."

"With great buns," Shelley added.

"Of course."

"And a good kisser."

"You modern women want it all, don't you?" George asked wryly.

Shelley shrugged. "Hey, as long as you're dreaming, you might as well dream of perfection."

"Yeah. Well, I'll leave the dreaming up to you. I've got work to do before I open my window."

"Yeah," Shelley agreed. "So do I." She tried to sound suitably reluctant about going to work, but secretly she was dying to pick up her stack of registered, certified and insured mail to see if Dr. Hunk had called to have his parcel put back on the truck for home delivery. "Thanks, George."

"No problem," George said, holding the heavy door open so she could precede him into the cavelike sorting room. In addition to the sorting bays, where she and her fellow mail carriers did the final sorting for their delivery routes, there were shelves for parcels that would be picked up at the postal windows and heavy canvas hampers where mail taken in was presorted for shipment to other post offices.

Shelley wove through a maze of the waist-high, wheeled hampers to reach the cubbyhole office of the Accountable Mail clerk, where she signed for the registered, certified and insured mail that she would attempt to deliver on her route. Each piece of this special mail was regulated at every phase of sorting and delivery; what she did not get a signature for while out on her route, she would return to the clerk at the end of the day.

She took the bundle of special mail to her sorting bay, then quickly riffled through it to see if the parcel for Dr. Booth had been put back into route delivery. It had.

Optimistic about her chances of actually getting a peep at Dr. Hunk before the end of the day, Shelley plunged into the task of sorting the regular mail.

Later, when she'd worked her way along her route to the institute, she found the iron gate open and the dogs nowhere in sight. Pulling her Jeep into the drive, Shelley parked halfway between the street and the house, then hiked to the front door.

The doorbell set off a chorus of barking inside, which was soon accompanied by the sound of approaching footsteps and a firm command for the dogs to calm down and sit. The door opened suddenly and Shelley found herself scarcely a yard away from a shaggy-haired man in a raggedy shirt, tattered cutoff jeans and the ugliest pair of eyeglasses she'd ever seen.

"Mail carrier," she said, holding the parcel within his view. "I have an insured parcel for Dr. Garrick Booth."

"I'm Dr. Booth."

"You are?" The question, sounding feeble and doubt-filled, slipped out before she realized she'd spoken aloud.

This was Dr. Hunk?

2

THE YOUNG WOMAN WHO'D brought the mail to the door didn't seem particularly disposed to relinquishing custody of it. Gere pushed his glasses higher on the bridge of his nose, hoping the box contained the new pair he'd special ordered. "Do you require identification?" he asked.

"Just your signature," she said, shoving the parcel and a pen toward his chest. "Sign next to the X."

Gere scribbled his name. "Now what?"

The young woman took the package back, ripped off the perforated card he'd just signed and returned the box to him. She held out a bundle of letters folded into a magazine. "These are yours, too." Smiling, she added, "Today's mail. This'll save you the hike to the mailbox."

As Gere took the bundle of envelopes, he was no longer thinking of mail at all. Every ampere of his considerable power of concentration was focused on the sight of the woman in front of him—on her smile, and all the dramatic transformations it effected on her face. With a research scientist's attention to detail, he noted the warm twinkle in her eyes, the upward curl of the corners of her mouth. He noticed the plumpness the gesture added to her cheeks, and the fullness of the lips.

She spoke, and even her voice seemed influenced by the smile. It was warmer, more melodic. "Have a nice day, Dr. Booth."

She turned and walked away. His observations didn't cease, they merely changed focus. Now he observed the whole of her. Her golden hair captured the sun in an intriguing way. She moved with an efficient economy of motion, yet her brisk stride was graceful. Her bottom was perfect—alluring and round under her tailored shorts. Her legs were beautifully muscled and smooth; sturdy, but sleek.

Gere liked what he saw; liked the total and the individual elements of the whole; was drawn to it in a way that was mysterious and visceral. It was a little like being punched in the gut without warning—and it was a little bit wonderful. He staggered under the impact and ambled out the front door, involuntarily moving in her direction without even realizing that he was doing so.

Sensing his approach from behind, she paused and turned. "Is there a problem?"

Awareness returned to Gere like a whack on the side of the head. What was he supposed to say to this woman? She had asked him a question. She would expect an answer.

He felt the worst kind of fool. He hadn't the vaguest idea what to say. Luckily, Wigglesworth and von Frisch dashed out of the house past Gere to investigate the stranger in their yard.

The woman gasped, then froze as they sniffed her shoes, her ankles, her knees. "They won't bite, will they?" she asked warily.

Relieved to have something to say, Gere replied, "They're just curious." He started to add an apology, but the woman didn't seem to mind the dogs. She was holding out her hand for them to smell.

"You're used to dogs," he said.

"I'm a mail carrier," she told him. "Dogs are an oc-
cupational hazard."

There seemed to be nothing else to say as she knelt
to pet the animals, and his beloved Dalmatians surrendered themselves to her attention with a shocking lack
of dignity. Gere glanced down at the mail in his hand
and caught sight of an odd-size, butter-yellow envelope. He didn't have to see the handwriting on the front
to know that it was addressed to Dr. Hunk, didn't have
to lift it to his nose to know that it would smell like the
perfume counter of a department store. How long
would he be receiving replies to that infernal ad?

A terrible thought occurred to him. A dire possibility. If this woman always delivered his mail, she probably had noticed the letters. What must she think?
What would she have been thinking when she was
standing on his doorstep sounding so official?

"Are you . . . Do you deliver the mail every day?"

She looked up at him. "Monday through Friday. My
sub delivers on Saturday."

*He just figured out that I've seen the Dr. Hunk let-
ters*, Shelley thought. His embarrassment was obvious, his shyness endearing.

"What are their names?" she asked, turning her attention back to the dogs, deliberately changing the
subject.

"Wigglesworth and von Frisch," he said.

"How unusual."

"They were named for entomologists."

"Oh." She rose. "You, uh . . . study bugs, huh?"

The corner of his mouth twitched almost into a smile.
"Yes. I study bugs."

He really wasn't so bad looking, Shelley reflected. He was just a bit . . . unkempt. "My brother buys crickets by the dozens," she said.

"Crickets?"

"For his reptiles."

"Is he a herpetologist?"

She laughed. "No. He's just a kid who likes lizards."

"I see. And his lizards eat crickets."

"Usually. But Annabel—she's always been finicky—hasn't eaten in over a week. Kevin's awfully worried about her. She's starting to look pretty puny. Kevin got her some meal worms, but she refused them, too."

"That's too bad."

Shelley shrugged her shoulders. "It happens, I guess. Reptiles can be finicky."

"I'm doing some work with frogs." He couldn't believe he'd told her that. He seldom volunteered information about his work, because he hadn't found many people outside the tight community of scientists who were the least bit interested in anything he did.

"Frogs? Really?"

She didn't seem to be as repelled by the nature of his work as most people. That pleased him, but he suddenly felt self-conscious. "It's nothing complicated."

A brief silence followed. Then Shelley bobbed her head toward the garden hose coiled next to a water spigot near the corner of the house. "Would you mind if I washed my hands before I leave? I don't want the rest of the mail I deliver today to smell like puppy dogs."

He gave her a blank look. "Wash your...? Of course. You can go inside to a bathroom, if you like."

She went over to the faucet. "This'll be quicker. I just need to rinse them off."

"Let me help." His hand collided with hers as she reached for the faucet knob. He drew his hand back, reaching instead for the nozzle end of the hose. "This nozzle attachment is tricky."

She straightened after turning on the water, just in time for a demonstration of the nozzle's most prevalent peccadillo: a tendency to go from a drip to Niagara Falls force unexpectedly. Squealing in surprise, she leaped backward, crossing her arms over her chest, futilely shielding herself from the spray that had already soaked her knit shirt—a white knit shirt that now clung wetly to her midriff and outlined something lacy on her chest.

Something lacy wasn't all it revealed. Mortified, mystified, mesmerized, Gere pointed the nozzle toward the ground. "I'm sorry." It seemed so inadequate, so unsubstantial, that he repeated it. "I'm sorry."

"No big deal," she said. "It was just water."

He looked at her face, to see if her cheerful tone was genuine, and found no anger. In fact, to his consternation, she smiled.

"It'll dry in no time in this heat," she told him.

Gere worked with the nozzle until he had established a gentle, steady flow. "Want to try again?"

She put her hands into the stream of water, scrubbing them together—sluicing the water halfway up to her elbows and then spontaneously splashing some over her face.

Gere, whose mind was usually more prone to scientific riddle than fantasy, found himself imagining her cavorting in a waterfall in a tropical setting, wet and sleek, in some kind of translucent white dress that clung to her. The images were so vivid in his mind that he responded physically to it—and was shocked by the intensity of his reaction. *Oh, Lord, what if she noticed?*

"That's enough," she said.

Could she possibly have read his mind? he wondered. Or noticed his reaction? If so, her face didn't show it. With an abrupt nod of acknowledgement, Gere pointed the hose down and turned around to close the faucet. With great trepidation, he chanced a quick look to check how obvious his dilemma was. His problem was not as noticeable as he'd feared—attributable in part to the genius of design that put a bulky fly flap over the heavy metal zipper now pressing into his flesh.

"Well, be seeing you," the woman said.

Gere walked with her to the truck. It was a standard mail Jeep with left-side steering, except that it had been painted white and had fancy red-and-blue scrollwork on the sides. "Is this a new design?" he asked.

"It's customized," she replied, settling into the driver's seat. "I own it."

"It looks official."

"It's postal service surplus. Contract carriers are responsible for their own vehicles. Most of us buy used postal service trucks at auction. Since we own them, we can do pretty much anything we want with them, as long as we have 'Mail' posted somewhere, and don't use the postal service eagle."

"Eagle?"

"The bald eagle. The official logo. It goes only on the vehicles owned by the postal service." She cranked the Jeep's engine and shrugged her shoulders. "I've got mail to deliver."

Five minutes. He'd first laid eyes on her five minutes ago, at the longest estimate. It wasn't long enough. He didn't want her to drive out of his life as though she'd never driven into it. "What's your name?" he asked.

She smiled. "Shelley Peters."

"Garrick Booth," he said, holding out his right hand.

She seemed surprised by the gesture and hesitated before extending her own hand. "It's still damp," she warned.

Gere didn't mind the dampness. He liked the feel of her hand—cool, smooth, soft, small. He felt an almost irrepressible urge to bend over and kiss it—some remnant of primal instinct from the days of gallantry?—but instead shook it firmly. Then, reluctantly, he released it. "Goodbye, Shelley."

"Bye, Dr. Booth."

He watched her drive away, consumed with longing as the Jeep dissolved into a distant dot of white. "My friends call me Gere," he said aloud, to no one.

DESPITE THE REFRESHING drenching in Dr. Hunk's front yard, the unseasonable heat had Shelley feeling drained and depleted. By the time she finished her route, she was looking forward to getting home and standing under a tepid shower for about half an hour. But first she had to unload the Jeep, dump the outgoing mail she'd collected, check in with the Accountable Mail clerk, and fill out Attempted Delivery slips on parcels that had been too large for boxes at addresses where no one had been at home to accept them.

She went through her end-of-day routine as quickly as possible and made a beeline for the door, where she practically ran over Maggie Schmidt, who was entering with the cart of parcels she was off-loading from her Jeep. Maggie had been Shelley's best friend since their Barbie doll years. It had been Maggie who had encouraged Shelley to put in her application at the post office.

"Shelley!" Maggie greeted. Her cheeks were flushed becomingly from the heat, and her dark hair was damp and curling around the hairline. "I was hoping I'd catch you. Want to go to Angelo's tonight?"

"You're not going out with Charles?" Shelley asked, referring to Maggie's lastest beau.

Maggie pulled an exaggerated frown. "Charles who?"

"Uh-oh."

"I'm thinking of founding a chapter of Jerk Junkies Anonymous."

"I'll apply for membership," Shelley offered, thinking of the last man she'd dated more than once. Definitely a jerk. "Angelo's sounds great." *A thousand times better than spending Friday night at home, alone.* "Seven-thirty?"

Maggie nodded. "See you there." She gave the cart a shove in the direction of her sorting bay, then turned to look at Shelley again. "Hey—what happened with Dr. Hunk? Did you see him?"

"I saw him," Shelley said with a dismal sigh.

"Well?"

"He was . . . nice."

"Nice?" Maggie asked, clearly disappointed at the lackluster description.

Shelley sighed again. She didn't want to talk about Dr. Garrick Booth, in part because she plain didn't know what to say about him. He was so different. So strange.

"That's *all* you're going to say?" Maggie protested. "That he's *nice?"*

"He's just a nice, ordinary person, that's all. There's nothing else to tell."

"Nothing to tell? Shelley, is he a hunk, or isn't he?"

"Isn't."

"Ugly?"

"No!" Shelley frowned. "He's not ugly, he's . . . unkempt." She could tell Maggie was hot to leech her for details she couldn't provide. "Look, let's talk about it tonight, okay? I'm so sticky I feel like taking off my clothes and standing in front of the refrigerator."

"No kidding," Maggie agreed, catching the front of her shirt in her fist and fanning it back and forth. "It was hotter than the Fourth of July today." She pinned Shelley with a stern look. "But I want a full report tonight when we're cool and comfy at Angelo's."

Shelley laughed. "I should have taken notes."

Half an hour later she was standing in the shower letting the water wash over her, still wondering how she was going to satisfy Maggie's rabid curiosity about Dr. Garrick Booth. He wasn't a hunk, as she'd anticipated, but her encounter with him had left a slew of lingering impressions, all of them poignant: the timidity of his smile, the quaint chivalry of his manners, the haunting expression of loneliness in his eyes. How was she supposed to describe such a complex man?

She stepped out of the shower, wrapped herself in a towel and chortled softly. She didn't know why she was wasting time worrying about how to describe Dr. Booth—Maggie would worm the details out of her, one by one. Maggie had been worming secrets out of her since she'd tricked her into telling who her boyfriend was in the sixth grade.

Still wrapped in the towel, Shelley flung herself across her bed. She'd worry about what to tell Maggie when the time came. For the next hour she was going to stretch out and vegetate and think of nothing at all!

After a brief but very restorative catnap, she dressed for the evening. Angelo's was not a singles meat rack but, located in the boutique-and-eatery end of Seminole County, where Shelley and Maggie had grown up, it was a popular restaurant with a predominately young, urban-professional clientele. Shelley and Maggie usually went there on Friday or Saturday nights if neither of them had dates, and they always preened and fussed beforehand. A girl never knew who she might run into.

The two women attracted more than a few appreciative male glances when they walked into the restaurant. Shelley had curled and scrunched her hair and worn her sexiest lace-edged tights and an oversize ballerina shirt pulled off one shoulder. Maggie's more conservative look—a pin-striped cotton blouse belted into cuffed denim shorts, her short dark hair tamed into what Shelley had teasingly called the Betty Boop look—was flattering and equally eye-catching.

Dubbed the Gruesome Twosome by Shelley's older brother, the pair invariably created an interesting tableau when they went places together—Shelley, blond and fair and voluptuous; Maggie, dark and sleek and sophisticated. Shelley had always thought it was ironic that Maggie's shell of sophistication hid a heart as soft as warm marshmallows, while her own bubbly persona masked a strong streak of cautious pragmatism.

Angelo's had the ambience of an Italian garden, with a proliferation of semitropical foliage and wine-bottle candle holders. Arriving slightly ahead of the dinner date crowd, Shelley and Maggie lucked into a great corner table from which they had a terrific view of the other diners.

For a while, Shelley was able to divert Maggie's interest in Dr. Hunk by keeping her talking about the lastest man in her life to earn the designation of jerk— Charles. It was the same old story. Charles was immature, irresponsible and unwilling to make a commitment. He promised to call, and didn't; he showed up late for dates; he wanted to keep everything "cool"— cool meaning no strings, no commitment, no responsibility, no future.

"In short," Maggie summed up the woeful tale of love gone wrong, "he's your typical common jerk. The story of my romantic life."

Shelley tended to be cautious about dating, but she'd had her share of experiences with jerks, certainly enough to allow her to relate to Maggie's growing disillusionment with men and the dating scene. Raising her glass of wine—the one glass she allowed herself per evening—she toasted, "To men— Who needs 'em?"

Laughing, Maggie clinked her glass against Shelley's. "Hear, hear!"

Maggie took a sip of wine, then put her glass back on the table and propped her chin on her fist. "So. Now that we've established that we don't need men, I want to hear all about Dr. Hunk. Why *isn't* he a hunk?"

Shelley set her glass down with a resigned thunk. "He wore funny glasses, he was shaggy, and his clothes looked like Goodwill castoffs."

Maggie stopped nibbling on her bread stick. "I thought you said he was rich."

Shelley shrugged. "I guess being rich means you don't have to wear great clothes."

"But he was nice?"

"I told you. He was sweet. Very polite. Very bashful. He struck me as kind of . . . innocent."

Maggie's jaw dropped in disbelief. "Innocent? In this day and age?"

"I know it sounds strange. I mean, he's some kind of doctor, and a famous scientist, and he was wearing a Harvard shirt—"

"I thought you said his clothes were ratty."

"Harvard shirts get ratty after they've been washed, just like any others. The seal was cracked, and the color was faded, and the sleeves were cut out, but it definitely said Harvard."

"Wow! I've never met anybody who actually *went* to Harvard."

"So you'd think that . . . It doesn't seem like he'd be . . . innocent."

"Maybe he's one of those absentminded-professor types."

Shelley gnawed her bread stick thoughtfully. He *had* seemed rather distracted. "Maybe so." She nodded. "I think you're right. That describes him pretty well."

"You want to know what I think?" Maggie said, abruptly laying down her salad fork.

Neither of them had spoken since the waiter brought their salads, so Shelley had no idea what path Maggie's thoughts had taken during their silence. "About what?" she asked.

"About this Dr. Hunk guy," Maggie said. "I think you like him."

"I've hardly met him," Shelley pointed out.

"I think you *really* liked him."

Shelley shook her head in firm denial. "It wasn't like *that*. He was nice enough to talk to, but he's not somebody I'd go *out* with."

"Why not?"

"He's not . . . I'm not sure he even noticed that I'm a woman."

"You mean he's—?"

"How would I know? I didn't get that impression. I just can't imagine him—" She giggled. "You know."

"Making love?"

"Going out on a date," Shelley replied, with a sniff of exasperation.

Maggie had resumed eating her salad. She swallowed a mouthful, then asked, "Why not?"

"He's just not the type."

"Bet you could change his mind if you tried."

Shelley frowned. "Look, Maggie, I've had this route four months and I've seen him exactly once. Even if I wanted to go out with him—which I don't—I doubt if I'd get the chance to try to change his mind. Now, can we change the subject, please?"

Maggie shrugged. "Sure." Leaning forward, she said in a confidential whisper, "Did you happen to notice that our waiter has great buns?"

"I liked his breadsticks, myself," Shelley quipped, lifting one from the breadbasket and taking a bite.

GERE WAITED IMPATIENTLY for Kelsey's hello on the other end of the line. "Kelsey?"

"Gere?"

"I want you to send me a letter."

"What time is it?"

"If you send it certified return, then I'll have to sign for it."

"It's after midnight, Gere. I was sound asleep. And tomorrow is Sunday. The post office is closed on Sunday." The sound of a yawn traveled through the line. "Didn't you get enough letters from the ad?"

"If I have to sign for it, then she'll have to bring it to the door."

He'd succeeded in waking her up. Suddenly actively interested in the conversation, she asked, "Who'll have to bring it to the door?"

"Shelley Peters."

"You're losing me, Gere. *Who* is Shelley Peters?"

"My mailman."

"I hope you mean mail *lady*," Kelsey retorted wryly.

"I suppose," Gere replied thoughtfully. "Although they call themselves 'carriers' now, don't they? Sounds rather like those people who harbor the typhoid virus, doesn't it?"

"Don't change the subject on me," Kelsey said firmly. "What does this Shirley—"

"Shelley."

"What does *Shelley* look like?"

"Look like?" He should have known Kelsey would turn nosy on him. "She looks like a woman, of course. Her hair shines, and she has... Her chest is quite nice."

Kelsey burst out laughing. "I can't tell you how delighted I am to hear that you noticed!"

"You shouldn't laugh at me," Gere said defensively. "I need your help."

"Let me get this straight. You want me to mail you a certified letter so that your mail carrier—who has shiny hair and great pecs—will have to knock on your door?"

"Will you do it?"

"Of course, I'll do it." Her yawn was audible over the phone line. "You don't mind if I wait until the post office opens?"

"You have a peculiar sense of humor, Kelsey."

"So I've been told. I'll write you a letter and mail it on the way home from school Monday, I promise."

"Thanks."

"Gere?"

"What?"

"Work with me on this. Go to the nearest mall and get yourself a decent haircut and some shirts."

"The mall?"

"You've seen malls," Kelsey said. "Lots of stores under a single roof. Air-conditioned. You'll like it. Stick to the stores playing rock music and you'll do okay."

Gere drummed his fingers on the tabletop after hanging up the phone. If Kelsey mailed the letter on Monday, and the letter took two days to reach the local post office, then it would be Wednesday at the earliest before Shelley delivered it. That was too long. Much too long. He should have told Kelsey to send the letter express.

He toyed with the idea of calling Kelsey back, but decided against it. If he woke her up again, she might not do it at all.

3

GERE WAS IN THE YARD with the Dalmatians when Shelley arrived with the mail on Monday. His face breaking into a smile, he waved a neon-orange Frisbee in greeting as she sidled the Jeep alongside the mailbox.

The floral scent that wafted into the air as she returned his greeting while holding his day's mail reminded Shelley of the three perfume-soaked letters addressed to Dr. Hunk in the stack. She crammed the envelopes into the box and flipped the lid shut, giving it a thump with the heel of her hand when the clasp proved stiff, then glanced again in Dr. Booth's direction.

She'd thought, from the eagerness of his greeting, that he might be coming over to chat, but he'd walked off toward the house, instead. Ignoring a niggle of disappointment, Shelley looked over her shoulder for approaching traffic, ready to reenter the highway.

All clear. She eased her foot off the brake.

"No! Shelley! Stop!"

She slammed on the brakes. Dr. Booth was jogging across the lawn, still holding the neon-colored Frisbee in one hand and carrying a small box with a suitcase-type handle in the other.

The Dalmatians, excited by his burst of movement, dashed out to meet him, loping and leaping, and sniffing curiously at the box. After dodging them for several yards, and almost tripping over them, he stopped long enough to hurl the Frisbee to the far corner of the lawn. He was winded when he reached the fence and swung an arm over the top, holding out the box. "I have something for you."

The gesture was so spontaneous and childlike that he seemed at least a decade younger than he had when she'd seen him on Friday, in part because his hair was shorter and, while disheveled from the wind, more stylishly cut. Perhaps it was the color of exertion in his cheeks that made Shelley notice that he had great cheekbones.

She switched off the engine of her Jeep and moved to get out. "What is it?"

"Beetles," he replied.

Beetles? This guy really *was* weird.

"For Annabel."

"Annabel?" Suddenly all she could think of was Edgar Allan Poe, and "Annabel Lee," the poem she'd memorized in tenth grade: *In her sepulcher there by the sea—in her tomb by the side of the sea.*

Dr. Booth and Edgar Allan Poe. It wasn't a reassuring association when she also remembered how isolated she was from civilization. She could see the headlines now: Mail Carrier Found Slain on Rural Highway; Body Mysteriously Gnawed by Beetles. Local Mad Scientist Sought for Questioning.

"Your brother's lizard," the mad scientist said.

"Huh?"

"The lizard that won't eat. Didn't you say her name was Annabel?"

"Oh." Shelley felt her face heating in embarrassment. "Of course. Annabel."

"She might like these."

"Oh. Sure." She took the box rather gingerly by the handle. It was plastic, with fine mesh windows. The inside was dotted with crawly little armored black bugs. "What kind are they?"

"Some common beetles I found. You wouldn't recognize the Latin name. My frogs are particularly fond of them."

"Your frogs?"

"I believe I mentioned that I was doing a diet study with frogs."

"Oh. Yes. You did," Shelley agreed.

"I've been offering them a variety of bugs to see which ones they like, or conversely, don't like."

Shelley thought for a long moment before asking, "Why?"

"Chemicals."

Her bewilderment must have been apparent, because he launched into an explanation. "Insects are filled with chemicals, and up to now, scientists have never made a concerted effort to identify these naturally-occurring chemicals or investigate their possible potential for the good of mankind."

"You mean like . . . medicine?"

He smiled delightedly, both at her interest and at her quick comprehension. "Yes. Like medicine. But that's only the beginning. Who knows what we might find, what we might be able to use. Natural insect control. Natural fertilizers. Miracle fibers. Ways of controlling our environment and improving quality of life without destroying the planet. We've been using plants for centuries, and we've hardly scratched the surface there. We're in a scientific Stone Age when it comes to insects."

"What does this have to do with frogs?" Shelley asked, after a brief silence.

"It could be the taste of specific chemicals that attracts frogs to certain bugs—or makes certain bugs unappealing. When I find a bug the frogs routinely gobble down or uniformly reject, then I check those bugs for unusual chemicals."

"Hmm," Shelley said, peering into the box. "And your frogs like these guys?"

"They're their favorite. Perhaps Annabel will like them, too. It's worth a try."

It struck her then what a remarkable, thoughtful thing it was for him to have done—to remember not only her brother's finicky lizard, but to remember the lizard's name. To have remembered *her* name. "I'll take them to Kevin after work," she said, with profound gratitude. "Thank you, Dr. Booth."

Her voice soothed his soul. The four hours he'd spent on hands and knees with a magnifying glass, sifting through grass and weeds, seemed but a small price to pay for such appreciation.

His response to her defied logic. He realized suddenly that he could *smell* her from across the five-foot space between them; that his olfactory sensors had isolated the light scent of something feminine and unique, the scent already firmly associated with her in his mind. From the air—air filled with pollens, smoke and the airborne particles of thousands of contaminants and exhausts emitted from automobile tailpipes and belched from the stacks of factories and refineries—his sensors had picked out the soap or shampoo or powder that made Shelley Peters smell like Shelley Peters. The concept fascinated him almost as much as the woman who was the catalyst for this phenomenon.

He'd always marveled at the idea that insects found each other by scent; to experience the same phenomenon, albeit on a much larger scale, left him flabbergasted.

"You got new glasses," she said, oblivious to the fact that he was in the throes of an unsettling experience.

Gere raised his hand to the sturdy frames. "Yes. These were inside the insured parcel you delivered yesterday." He grinned self-consciously. "No more tape."

"Nice," she said. The dark, tortoise-shell frames were too heavy to be truly fashionable, but they were brusquely masculine, and strangely compatible with his no-nonsense demeanor.

A silence ensued, grew long, threatened to become awkward. "Well," Shelley said. "I've got mail to deliver. Thanks again for the beetles, Dr. Booth. If Annabel likes them, it'll probably save her life."

"Shelley?"

The gravity of his tone drew her attention. She hoped he wasn't going to warn her that the beetles would bite.

"Please call me Gere."

"Gere?"

"Short for Garrick."

Shelley's face broke into a huge smile as she nodded. "Sure."

GERE JERKED TO AWARENESS like a sleeper awakened by the jangle of a loud alarm. He checked his watch and shouted, "Oh, damn!"

He'd planned to be outside with the Frisbee fifteen minutes before Shelley's usual arrival time. Now he'd missed her. Just in case, he dashed from the greenhouse, through the kitchen of the house, into the living room. He reached the front window in time to see her

Jeep dissolve into a dot of white in the distance. He stood there, hands jammed into the back pockets of his new denim shorts, and stared at the desolate highway while disappointment gnawed a hollowness inside him.

The squeak of her brakes. He had an uncanny ability to tune out distractions as he worked—barking dogs, heat, cold, hunger pangs, ticking clocks, whirring motors, even ringing telephones. But today, even when he was so absorbed in his work that he'd lost track of time, the distant squeak of brakes had registered in his brain with the effect of a clanging alarm. How had his mind recognized that sound, linked it with her? He couldn't have heard it more than twice, and not noticed it when he did—yet his mind had made the association and picked out that sound from among all others to hear.

Exactly as he'd been able to perceive her scent yesterday.

Selective perception: the mind's tendency to pick out stimuli related to a specific need. The smell of food when you're hungry. A mother's heightened sensitivity to a baby's middle-of-the-night cries. He remembered the term from the introductory psychology course he'd taken as an undergraduate. What specific need was setting off alarms in his mind when he heard her brakes squeak? When he smelled her perfume from five feet away?

The question intruded on his work for the rest of the day—and on his sleep that night. "Tomorrow," he groaned into his pillow, before giving it a savage, futile punch. *Tomorrow he wouldn't lose track of the time.*

He was outside half an hour before her usual arrival time. Though he'd brought the Frisbee out, even the dogs tired of the game quickly in the midafternoon heat, so he contented himself with sitting Indian-style on the shaded porch, watching a crown spider put the final touches on a web she was weaving between the side of the house and the branch of a variegated box shrub.

Wigglesworth and von Frisch leaped up, alerting him to Shelley's approach seconds before the telltale squeal of her brakes. Gere rose and dusted the seat of his denim shorts before sauntering out to meet her. She turned off the Jeep's engine and got out, walking toward the fence as he approached from the opposite side. Holding up a clipboard, she smiled. "I need your autograph again, Doctor—" She almost said Hunk, but caught herself, and corrected, "Er, Gere."

He tried to sound surprised. "Oh?"

"Certified letter," she explained.

"Hmm!"

Hmm, indeed, she thought, more perplexed than ever. It was not a perfumed letter addressed to Dr. Hunk. It was a rather official-looking business-size envelope addressed to Garrick Booth, Ph.D., postmarked from a small town in Indiana. The return address, in a no-nonsense block type, was: National Society of Professional Male Strippers.

Gere signed where he was supposed to sign, glanced at the envelope and turned several shades of red to purple. His lip compressed into a tight line, and a muscle twitched in his jaw.

"Don't shoot me, I'm only the messenger," Shelley said lightly.

Gere's gaze leveled on hers. "Shooting's not my style. I bury people in anthills, or slip roach eggs into the counters or under their sinks."

Shelley's eyes widened.

"That was a joke," he said. "I don't really bury people in anthills."

Her eyes narrowed suspiciously. "What about the roach eggs?"

He glanced at the letter in his hand meaningfully. "A distinct possibility."

Dead silence followed. Shelley was consumed by curiosity. Certified letters were not uncommon, but usually they were sent by people who needed a formal record that a piece of mail had been sent. Who had sent him the certified letter? And what was the story behind all the Dr. Hunk envelopes? She was dying to ask, but she dared not. As a mail carrier, she was supposed to deliver the mail, not question it. And as a fellow human being, she simply didn't know him well enough to intrude in his private business.

"I'm not a male stripper," he said awkwardly.

His embarrassment touched her. Again, she sensed a quality of innocence about him, a vulnerability. The thought of this man—this shy recluse—getting up in front of a crowd and taking off his clothes to bump-and-grind music was ludicrous.

"I didn't think you were."

He dropped his gaze to the top of his sneaker and gave a little half nod.

It was so solemn, that nod. Had he wished— dreamed, *hoped*—somewhere in the back of his mind, that she—that *anyone*—might believe that he got up in front of women and became an object of sexual adoration?

Of course, he did. He was human, after all. What man wouldn't want a woman to believe it possible? What woman, even the most proper and prim, wouldn't like to think, although it would never happen, that a man would believe it possible she could become an object of male fantasy and lust?

"I've seen those gag envelopes before," she said, in a chipper, upbeat voice, hoping to convince him that she knew it was a hoax because of the envelope, and not because she didn't believe it possible that he could stand up in front of women and take off his clothes if he chose to.

"Gag envelopes?"

"Sure. They sell them at party stores and card shops. Professional Society of Male Strippers. National Alliance for the Reformation of Sexual Perverts. Association of Survivors of Sexually Transmitted Diseases."

"I'll probably get one of those next week," he said grimly. After an awkward stretch of silence, he added, "I guess you see a lot of . . . *interesting* mail.

"Oh, sure," Shelley replied. "All kinds." She deduced from the fact that he was staring pensively at his sneaker again that he was thinking about the Dr. Hunk letters, just as she was, and searched for a way to change the subject. Then she realized she hadn't told him about Kevin's lizard.

"Annabel loved the beetles," she said.

He risked a glance at her face. "She did?"

"She stared at them a few minutes, tried one and then went on a beetle binge. Kevin thinks you may have saved her life."

"Good," he said, with a gentle smile. "I'm glad."

"If she'd died, Kevin would have been devastated. He's at one of those awkward ages, and, well . . . you know how it is for boys and their pets."

"How old is he?"

"Eleven." She grinned at his reaction. "I know. It's quite an age gap. He was one of those surprise babies.

My mother was so pregnant she had to waddle into my older brother's high school graduation ceremony. It was a family joke that she would probably give birth while the band was playing 'Pomp and Circumstance.'"

"How many of you are there?"

"Four. There's Ron—he's a mechanic for the city motor pool—and then there's Lizzy—she had a baby in July—and then there's me—all I deliver is the mail."

"The mail's important," Gere said.

Shelley flashed him an indulgent smile. "Not nearly as important as a grandbaby—at least as far as my parents are concerned. And of course, Kevin is proud as punch to be the only uncle in his elementary school."

She'd told him just enough to pique his interest in her even more. He wanted to ask if she wanted children, if she had a man she loved, what had inspired her to become a mail carrier.

"I have a sister," he said. "She's the one who sent me this letter."

"She must have an interesting sense of humor," Shelley remarked, wondering why it was such good news that his *sister* had sent the letter.

"She has a *quirky* sense of humor." He sighed softly, then added gravely, "She says I don't have a sense of humor at all."

"You?"

He grinned. "Thank you."

"For what?"

"For believing that I might have one."

"Everyone has a sense of humor. Maybe yours is just different from your sister's."

"I didn't bust anything laughing over this return address."

"That? That's more of a groaner than a laugh."

"I cringed."

"Close enough," she said. "Speaking of return addresses—"

"You have mail to deliver." Gere hoped he didn't sound as bereft as he felt at the thought of her leaving. His ploy of the certified letter might have backfired because of Kelsey's perverse humor, but he'd had the opportunity to talk to Shelley. The problem was, it wasn't enough. These five-minute interfaces were enough to tease and frustrate, enough to whet the appetite—and far less than enough to satisfy it.

He was going to have to resort to more radical measures. Possibilities were tumbling over methodically in his mind even as Shelley thanked him again for the beetles and waved goodbye. She was long gone before he remembered to open the letter from Kelsey. He did so and thought, *Big Brother isn't dead; he's just had a sex change.*

For there, on the gag stationery, in flowing blue script, his omniscient, all-knowing, all-seeing big sister had written: "It's time to ask her out on a date."

4

As soon as he spied Shelley's Jeep, Gere tossed the Frisbee to the far corner of the yard and jogged out to the fence to greet her.

"Hi!" she replied, cutting the vehicle's engine. "You must be expecting this." She held out her clipboard.

"What is it?"

"Another certified letter. National Organization of Tormented Hemorrhoid Sufferers." She managed a straight face, but just barely. "Postmarked Indiana."

Frowning, Gere took the clipboard and muttered, "The only pain in my backside is my sister." He wielded the pen with such pressure that the paper ripped, which embarrassed him even more than the letter. "Sorry," he grumbled, picking at the torn strip of paper with his thumbnail, trying futilely to straighten and realign it.

"No problem," Shelley said, retrieving the clipboard. She ripped the certified return form from the back of the envelope, then removed the envelope from the clipboard and, leaning forward, handed the letter back to Gere. "The signature's legible. That's all that matters."

"Umm," Gere muttered. Though they were on opposite sides of the fence, he was keenly aware of how little actual distance separated them. He was standing, and she was seated in the Jeep, which gave him a new angle of observation, especially when she leaned forward. His eyes settled on the silver pendant that settled

cozily in the modest cleavage at the V of her shirt as she
returned to driving posture. The filigree heart seemed
to have a life of its own as it rode the subtle rise and fall
of her chest. Gere thought he might not mind being a
clump of silver if he could dangle at the end of a chain
and sit right there, between Shelley Peters's breasts,
touching her intimately, absorbing her warmth.

"Gere?"

He snapped to attention with the mortified expression of a child caught daydreaming in class. "I'm
sorry— Did you say something?"

"Here's the rest of your mail."

Gere reached for the stack of envelopes and sales
brochures she was holding out. "Thanks."

Shelley sensed that he had something on his mind,
and waited for him to bring it up, but he remained peculiarly silent. Finally, she started the Jeep's engine.
"Well . . ."

Here it was, Gere thought. The moment for truth. For
action. It was now or never—or at the very least, tomorrow. He didn't want to wait another day. He
wouldn't wait another day.

"Would you like to go to dinner with me Saturday
night?" he blurted out.

It was the last thing in the world she'd expected him
to say. Shocked, Shelley looked at him as though he'd
suggested she paint her face purple and participate in
some pagan tribal ritual.

She cut her engine. "Dinner?"

Dinner? With Dr. Hunk, the bug hermit? Did she
want to go to dinner with Dr. Hunk? Dinner, as in a
date?

He was nice, but—

"Saturday night," he repeated.

Shelley's mind raced. It was only dinner. It wasn't as though he'd suggested . . . anything suggestive. He was lonely; she'd always thought so. He was reaching out to her, human being to human being. He just wanted companionship, company.

But did she want to encourage him?

She remembered the beetles he'd given her for Annabel. He'd saved Annabel's life, and Kevin would have been devastated if Annabel had died. She owed him.

She'd have spent a month of Saturday nights sitting at home if she could have had some dynamite plans for *this* Saturday night. If she'd had unbreakable plans, she could have turned him down with a clear conscience. But the abysmal truth was, she had *zip* planned for Saturday night.

Wavering between acceptance and refusal, she looked up at his face. Never had she seen a person's features so totally involved in expressing one emotion: hope. His eyes sparkled with it, his lips were tremulous with it. Shelley had a sneaking suspicion he might be involuntarily holding his breath while he waited for her answer. She hadn't seen such earnest yearning on a male face since Buddy Walker had invited her to the homecoming dance in her freshman year at high school.

Shelley felt a warmth spreading in her chest. Her heart melting, no doubt. No woman with an ounce of human compassion would have been able to squelch such hope on a man's face, especially a man as endearingly sincere as Dr. Garrick Booth. "I'd love to go to dinner with you," she said.

She watched his struggle for control as he absorbed her acceptance, witnessed the loss of the battle as his lips twitched into a wide, far-too-revealing smile of genuine pleasure. He had good teeth—large, white and

perfectly aligned—and, she noticed for the first time, a
rather sensual mouth, with nicely shaped lips.

Seduced by his guilelessness and warmed by the
flattery of his blatant attraction, she found herself
smiling back as she started the Jeep's engine.

Gere waited until she was out of sight before opening the letter. One thing about his sister: She was a
woman who knew how to make a point. In this case,
the words were: "Wear a suit and don't forget the after-
shave I gave you for Christmas."

ANOTHER DATELESS FRIDAY night, another dinner at
Angelo's with Maggie. This time their table was in the
middle of the room, and between waiters and entering
and exiting diners, the aisles around them had as much
foot traffic as the interstate had vehicles. It was after
ten, and they'd just finished dinner. The waiter had
cleared their table except for coffee cups and wine-
glasses and had handed them dessert menus.

"Are we having dessert?" Maggie asked. "We probably walked off at least a cannoli each at the mall."

Shelley studied the menu and sighed wistfully. "I'm
not in the mood for cannoli."

"Want to halve a piece of cheesecake?"

"The chocolate-chip cheesecake with hot-fudge top-
ping?"

"We didn't do *that* much walking!" Maggie said.

"You're right," Shelley conceded. "Besides, I'll probably have something sinfully rich tomorrow night."

"Go ahead. Rub it in. You've got a date for Saturday
night with a man who's taking you to a fancy restaurant."

"You've got a date this week, too," Shelley reminded
her.

"Oh, yeah. A fix-up. I'm going to my sister-in-law's Thursday night so she can introduce me to the son of a woman she works with. Big deal!"

"It could turn out to be something."

"Yeah. A disaster. The way every other blind date I've ever had has turned out. I won't even get a decent meal out of it. My sister-in-law is a lousy cook."

The waiter returned and picked up the menus. "Well, ladies?"

"Chocolate-chip cheesecake," they replied in unison.

"Maybe your brother will grill steaks," Shelley said, as the waiter disappeared.

"It won't be Gaspard's."

Shelley shrugged. "It's only dinner."

"With Dr. Hunk. To Gaspard's. Shelley, a man doesn't take a woman to the fanciest restaurant in five counties unless he's trying to impress her."

Shelley propped her chin on her hand and sighed. "The man's a hermit, Maggie. He probably didn't know where to go. He probably called the chamber of commerce or checked AAA for a recommendation."

Maggie cocked an eyebrow. "And I suppose you're not trying to impress him, either?"

"No!"

"And that's why you spent four hours at the mall frantically trying on clothes, and *nothing* was good enough."

"You can't wear just anything to Gaspard's. It requires a certain look, and I just don't have anything suitable."

"What about your little black dress?"

"Too little."

Maggie gave her a puzzled look. "You haven't gained weight. That dress fits you like a glove."

"Oh, it fits," Shelley agreed. "There's just *too little* of it. It's too short at the bottom and too low at the neck. I need something so tasteful it'll make people gag."

"And you're not trying to impress him," Maggie said ironically.

"I'm not trying to impress him. But I don't want to be an embarrassment to him, either."

"Wear your black dress."

Shelley shook her head adamantly. "Too flashy. I need something conserv—" She stopped abruptly.

"What?" Maggie asked.

"I just remembered where I might get the perfect dress." She put her napkin on the table and stood. "Excuse me."

"Shelley, where—?"

"I've got to make a phone call," Shelley replied over her shoulder. She wove through the crowded dining room to the phones located along the back wall near the rest rooms. Between the lilting background music and the din of the diners' conversations, she had to put her hand over her left ear to hear through the receiver at her right.

"Lizzy?" she said, when her sister answered the phone. "Shelley. Sorry to call so late, but it's sort of an emergency. Remember that dress—"

She was smug with accomplishment when she rejoined Maggie at their table. "Mission accomplished. I pick up the dress in the morning."

"What dress are you talking about?"

"The one Lizzy bought when Joshua's great aunt died two years ago. They had to leave in such a hurry that she didn't have time to shop, so she bought the first thing suitable for a funeral. She never really liked it because it was too drab. I was afraid she might have donated it to charity, but she still has it."

"And you want to wear this dress on a date?"

"It's perfect," Shelley said. "It's dark, it's got a high neck and long sleeves. It's very tasteful."

"You're weird about this guy, Shelley."

"I am not!" Shelley said. "I don't even know why I agreed to go, except that he looked so ... He was so sincere when he asked, and I didn't want to hurt his feelings."

"Shel-ley," Maggie prodded, giving her a look of total consternation. "Is this a mercy date?"

"No!" Shelley snapped. "Of course not. You know I don't *do* mercy dates." She fixed Maggie's face with a pointed stare. "Unlike one person I know, who keeps letting her big, soft heart get her into dead-end situations with men who aren't worth the trouble."

Maggie ignored the old, familiar nagging. "Then what, exactly, do you call it when you don't know why you're going out on a date, except that you didn't want to hurt his feelings?"

Shelley had been wondering the same thing. "It's...a friend date," she said, trying to sound confident.

"A 'friend' date?" Maggie repeated skeptically.

Shelley decided she liked the sound of it. "Yes. A friend date. I don't feel...*you know*...about him, but Gere is a nice person, so why shouldn't I go to dinner with him?"

"So it's Gere, now, instead of Dr. Hunk?"

"I've never called him Dr. Hunk," Shelley replied, then qualified, "To his face."

"You called him Doctor something," Maggie said.

"Booth."

"And now it's Gere."

"His first name's Garrick."

Maggie was pensive a moment, then announced, "I still say you're weird about him."

"What's weird about friends calling each other by their first names?"

"The whole situation is weird. Did you ever find out why he was getting mail addressed to Dr. Hunk?"

"I haven't asked."

"And you're going out with him? How do you know he's not some kind of pervert?"

Shelley laughed at the notion. "Trust me, Maggie. He's no pervert. Whatever the story is, I don't think this Dr. Hunk business was his idea. If you knew him, you'd understand. He's so shy."

"Are you sure this guy's not doing a number on you, Shelley?"

"Positive," Shelley answered, then frowned as she propped her elbow on the table and her chin on her fist. "I'd be very disappointed if I found out he was just another jerk."

"Why should he be any different?" Maggie asked wryly.

"Because he's nice," Shelley said. "He's not a hunk, but he's . . . nice." Noting Maggie's skeptical expression, she added defensively, "Well, how many genuinely *nice* people are there left in the world?"

"Weird," Maggie declared, then grinned wickedly. "But don't worry, Shel. If it turns out he's not as nice as you think he is, you can become the second charter member of Jerk Junkies Anonymous."

THE NEXT MORNING, Shelley stood in front of the full-length mirror in her sister's Victorian bedroom and frowned. "I look like a Pilgrim."

"Why do you think I haven't worn it since the funeral?" Lizzy asked. She was propped up in her bed in a sea of cabbage roses and ruffle-and-lace-trimmed pillows, nursing her infant daughter. "When I bought it, I thought the white collar around the face would soften the effect—you know, make the black less harsh. However, if anything, it does the opposite."

Shelley stared at her reflection and sighed. "At least it's tasteful."

"Oh, it is that," Lizzy agreed. "It was perfect for a funeral. I'm not sure why you want it for a date."

"From what I've heard about Gaspard's, it's mostly an older crowd. Mostly millionaires. I don't want to wear anything flashy. I wouldn't want anyone pointing or whispering."

"Well, you'll blend in with that little number."

Shelley harrumphed at her reflection. "I guess. I just hope no one asks me if Plymouth Rock was slippery when I stepped off the gangplank of the *Mayflower*." She turned to face Lizzy. "You're the fashion authority. Do you think a necklace would help. Some pearls?"

"You could always get some black patent shoes with big buckles on them," Lizzy teased.

"If you weren't holding my favorite niece—" Shelley teased back.

"What?"

"Pillow fight!" Shelley said playfully.

"Not with my pillows!" Lizzy retorted. "Do you know how much goose-down pillows cost these days?"

Laughing, Shelley perched on the corner of the bed. "Do you think they were cheap back in our world-champion pillow-busting days?"

Lizzy smiled. Her face was similar to Shelley's, but a bit fuller, and she wore her light brown hair long so she could tie it into a ponytail at her nape. "It's a wonder mother didn't hang us up by our toenails!" she exclaimed.

"Well, now that we buy our own pillows, we have a new perspective on child discipline," Shelley said drolly. She reached out to caress her niece's tiny foot. "I suppose when little Brittany here goes through her pillow-fight stage, you're going to hang her up by these adorable toenails."

"Daily!" Lizzy said. "I considered it this morning when she decided she was hungry at five forty-five."

"You've spoiled her, feeding her anytime she sheds a few tears. From now on you should explain to her that the fountain is closed on Saturday morning before nine."

"Just what I need," Lizzy replied. "Advice straight from *The Maiden Aunt's Complete Guide to Child Rearing*."

"'Maiden aunt'?" Shelley feigned offense. "I'll remember you said that the next time you need a baby-sitter." Giving Brittany's foot one last tickle, she stood. "Right now, I'm going to get out of this dress so I can play with my favorite baby. Now that you've got her fat and happy, I'm going to spoil her rotten!"

Shelley stayed at Lizzy's until midafternoon, entertaining little Brittany while Lizzy caught up on her housework and ran some errands. Then she went home and did some dusting and polishing so everything would be tidy when Gere arrived.

Just before seven-thirty Shelley heard a car turn onto the drive and stole a glance out her bedroom window. She bit back a laugh when she saw the vehicle Gere was driving. *A VW Beetle convertible. Of course. What else would Dr. Hunk, the entomologist, drive?* Her laughter segued into a smile as she thought how her brother, the mechanic, would salivate when she told him her date drove a classic Volkswagen Beetle ragtop.

Gere unfolded from the driver's seat and walked in front of the car en route to her door. His dark suit, pristine white shirt and a Windsor-knotted tie made her glad she'd followed her instinct to dress conservatively. For a man whose usual appearance was reminiscent of a scruffy teddy bear, he looked surprisingly dapper. He walked with a confident gait, and his movements were fluid and graceful in a masculine way.

Stepping away from the window to wait for his knock, Shelley wondered why it should surprise her if he proved to have a certain level of social poise. He was, after all, an educated man, and from all indicators, probably well-off financially. For all she knew, he might eat at Gaspard's three nights a week!

That thought made her nervous. She wasn't totally unsophisticated, but she felt more at home in a cozy place like Angelo's than in a formal restaurant like Gaspard's. She hadn't accepted this date expecting a rollicking good time, however. She'd accepted it because it had seemed important to Gere, and he'd done her a big favor, and one good turn deserved another. After all, the gods of real-life love and romance did not issue princes to every hopeful princess wannabe every Saturday night. Smart aspiring princesses learned to accept the inevitability of keeping company with a few frogs along the way, and made the most of what fate presented.

At least Dr. Garrick Booth is a polite frog, she reflected, on her way to answer the front door. Unless her judgment was way off, he wasn't likely to mistake friendship for lust and make a wrestling match part of the after-dinner agenda. It should be a pleasant evening, if not an exciting one.

She went to the living room and waited impatiently for the ring of the doorbell. She heard the slam of a car door instead. The thought that he might have decided to turn tail and run flitted through her mind, then was dispelled by the sharp jangle of the bell. Shelley took in a deep breath, counted to ten slowly, then opened the door.

He'd brought flowers—a multicolored bouquet of mixed blossoms wrapped in lace-patterned cellophane, which he held out to her with the sober mien of a preadolescent in the throes of a bad case of puppy love. Except for his size and maturity, he could have posed for a classic vignette of a boy bringing a girl flowers for the first time, the expression in his eyes both pleading and determined.

Shelley experienced such a pang of tenderness for him that she would have kissed him on the cheek as she accepted the flowers had she not been afraid of embarrassing him. So she thanked him with a smile, smelled the flowers, exclaimed over their beauty, and asked if he'd had any trouble finding her house.

"None at all," he replied. "Your directions were excellent. The pelicans helped, once I found the street."

Shelley had a set of pressed-stone pelicans stationed like sentries at the end of the drive. "I had to do something to make my driveway stand out, since all the buildings are identical. My neighbor calls them Contemporary Cracker boxes."

"It doesn't look like a cracker box inside," Gere said, scanning the living room while Shelley arranged the flowers in a vase in the adjoining kitchen. "It's—"

It's just like you, he thought. *Neat. Pretty, without being frivolous. Unique.*

"Pleasant," he finished, feeling the inadequacy of the word. He should be saying that the room made him feel welcome and comfortable. He should be saying that he would feel very much at home here. He should tell her that the painting of the mother flamingo and her chicks touched his heart, and that the plump, contemporary sofa looked like it would be a comfortable place to stretch out at the end of a long day. He should tell her that the living room, with its warm beige walls, soft lighting and pots of trailing ivy would be a heavenly refuge on a stormy night, that he could imagine how it would be to cuddle her in his arms and listen to the rain on the roof and the roar of distant thunder and know that they were safe and dry and content in each other's company.

She brought the bouquet into the living room and set the vase on the coffee table. "Amazing how flowers brighten up a room, isn't it?"

"Hmm," he agreed, wishing he had the courage and quickness of tongue to tell her that it was her smile that brightened the room for him.

Two Ph.D.'s, and a pleasant "hmm" is the shining example of your conversational skills. Face it, Booth, when it comes to women, you're a social incompetent.

"Would you like something to drink before we go?" Shelley asked.

"Our reservations are for eight," he said regretfully. "Maybe we'd better—"

"Oh. Sure. I'll get my purse."

Once they were settled in the VW she said, "You might as well tell me about your car. When I tell Ron you have a classic VW convertible, he'll expect me to have specifics."

Who the hell is Ron? Gere wondered frantically, then remembered her mentioning an older brother. He stole a sideways glance at Shelley, who was digging in her purse. "Specifics?"

"Like what year it is, and what size engine it has. Ron's *really* into classics. He's the one who keeps my Jeep running." She'd located a pen and a small spiral notebook, which she opened to a fresh page. "Okay. Shoot."

Gere, grateful to have been presented with a convenient topic of conversation, gave her the information she wanted, while Shelley took notes. It didn't take long to exhaust the subjects of model and engine.

"It's in excellent condition," Shelley said, stuffing the notepad back into her purse.

"The original owner kept her garaged most of the time," Gere explained.

"What made you choose a classic? I mean, instead of a new car?"

Gere shrugged. "I bought my first one in college. Some idiot broadsided me and totaled my car, and I went shopping for another one. It was a joke at first. An entomology major, driving a Beetle. But I took it for a test drive." He smiled at the memory. "It was a beautiful spring day, and I put the top down, and when I got back to the lot, I bought it."

"A man and his car," Shelly said.

"I drove it for the next four years. Eventually it started dying a natural death. I was looking around for another one, when a friend of mine heard about this one. I guess if she ever wears out, I'll have to get a real car."

"My brother would say classics are the only real cars."

"You say he's a mechanic by trade?"

"Mmm-hmm. He's in the police-department motor pool. He keeps the cop cars rolling."

"And your sister?"

"She worked for the telephone company until she had a baby in July, so she's a full-time mommy for the time being."

"A baby," he said, as though the concept were unfathomable to him. It was. He had been only four when Kelsey was born and had only a young child's sketchy perceptions of a tiny being who cried a lot. There had been no more children in the family—no more siblings, and no cousins. Kelsey had been his only peer in a life populated by adults. "So you're an aunt."

"Yes." Shelley said. "More important, my mother is a grandmother. It kind of takes the pressure off, if you know what I mean."

"Your mother wanted grandchildren?"

"Doesn't every mother?" Shelley asked rhetorically. "She had about given up after Ron and his wife broke up, and neither Lizzie nor I was married, but then Lizzie met Joshua, and there was the wedding craziness, and then finally, all the baby planning."

Gere wondered if his own mother had ever suffered a pang of longing for grandchildren and decided she hadn't. Paulette Booth was not an unfeeling person, but following her husband's death, she had poured all her passion into her work, letting the love of science, which she had shared with him, fill all the spaces love was supposed to fill. It was not nearly as risky as trusting people to fill those spaces; people could die, and leave those spaces empty and aching. The work remained— challenging, demanding, rewarding.

Gere himself had never given a thought to children. Realizing that made him sad, somehow, just as thinking about his mother always made him sad.

Shelley exhaled a soft sigh. "Brittany is so sweet. I just hope Mother doesn't decide that one is so wonderful she needs to have a dozen more right away."

Gere chanced a sideways glance at her. "Don't you want children?"

Was it the wistfulness of that gentle little sigh that had made him ask such a personal question—and made him so certain of her answer?

"Sure, I do," she said, and smiled at the idea. "When I meet the right man and we decide together that the time is right."

Suddenly, Gere's collar seemed a bit too tight. "Oh."

"What about you?" she asked.

"What?" he questioned. Then remembering the current topic under discussion, he said, "You mean children."

Shelley nodded.

"I've never thought about it," he told her. *Until two minutes ago.* He was thinking about it now.

"I guess most men don't," Shelley said. "It must be a biological thing."

"Hmm," Gere agreed. "Hormonal influences, most likely." Was it his imagination, or was it getting warm inside the car?

"That's a horrible thought," Shelley said.

"Horrible?"

"Well, think about it! Babies are so ... sweet." She remembered the weight of Brittany in her arms. "They're so tiny, and yet so ... perfect. They're totally dependent on adults for survival, yet they're also very independent, and each one has a very individual personality. It's sad to think that anyone who's ever held a baby would want one just because of *hormones*."

"The entire emotional reaction is attributable to the basic survival instinct."

Shelley turned her head so she could see his face. "Survival instinct?"

"Yes. Survival. Without procreation, there would be no continuation of the line. Our desire to mate and reproduce grows out of the instinct to perpetuate ourselves through our offspring."

"That's not very romantic," Shelley observed. In fact, it was the singularly least romantic thing she'd ever heard.

Gere chuckled. "Romance is an invention of man, not biology."

"And love?" she challenged.

"The luxury of moving higher up the evolutionary ladder."

Sensing movement, he glanced over and saw that she had crossed her arms over her waist. "Hogwash!"

Gere cleared his throat. "That's ... uh, reduced to simplest terms, of course. Human beings are very complex, and therefore their emotions are..." His voice trailed off as he realized she didn't understand the point he was trying to make. Why didn't he just accept the fact that he didn't know how to communicate with nonscientists? He wanted so badly to make a good impression, and he'd succeeded only in offending her.

He was relieved to spy the restaurant, glad to have the diversion of maneuvering the car into the canopied entrance and dealing with the valet before trying to reestablish a comfortable rapport with Shelley.

From the first sight of the valet in his formal gray suit, Shelley dreaded going inside the restaurant. It didn't help any that her "nice guy" had shown signs of being an insensitive egghead. *Love a luxury of being higher on the evolutionary ladder?* Only someone with a Ph.D. could come up with a theory that screwy! She got out of the car when the valet opened the door for her, then waited in the arched entryway for Gere.

Again, as Gere walked toward her, she was impressed by how elegant he appeared in his dark suit. Personally, she felt like a Pilgrim who'd caught the wrong boat. Oh, to be at Angelo's in her little black dress instead of in this stuffy place in her Pilgrim dress with its stiffly starched collar!

He cupped her elbow as they crossed the entryway to the door, where a uniformed doorman gave them a formal, down-the-nose "Good evening," as he pulled open the heavy, paneled door.

A massive chandelier hung suspended from the high vaulted ceiling of the foyer, casting shadows on the pristine white, wainscoted walls, and massive Grecian-style pedestals held pots of ferns so large that the tips of the fronds brushed Gere's and Shelley's shoulders as they waited to be seated. Feeling a gentle squeeze on her elbow, Shelley turned her gaze to Gere's face. The seriousness of his expression drained all other thoughts from her mind.

"I tend to approach things from a scientific viewpoint," he said.

"I noticed."

"Sometimes it must make me seem . . . distant and clinical."

She peered into his eyes. He looked decidedly more vulnerable than clinical. She wanted to comfort him, but he didn't give her a chance before continuing. His voice was husky with intensity. "It doesn't mean that I don't feel, just like everybody else."

Her eyes never left his. "That, I believe."

5

SHELLEY HAD NEVER FELT another person's isolation, loneliness or desperate need for acceptance so acutely as she felt Gere's as she looked into his eyes in the foyer of that elegant restaurant. He was more guileless, even, than Kevin. She lifted her hand to caress his cheek, but the second her fingertips made the most tentative contact with his face, the maître d' returned to his station and wished them a good evening. She drew her hand back guiltily.

Gere turned to the tuxedoed head waiter. "Dr. Garrick Booth. I had reservations."

The maître d' nodded with a peculiar blend of obsequiousness and arrogance, and bid them follow him to a table. The Grecian-column theme was repeated throughout the dining room, with rows of the thick columns serving as space dividers that gave the impression of intimate dining alcoves rather than a single large room. Pots of ferns and vases of cut lilies perched on the columns—the green of the fern fronds and the stems of the lilies providing the only relief from the stark white walls and starched white tablecloths.

They were shown to a small round table that produced an immediate intimacy as they settled into their chairs. Shelley crossed her legs and slanted them to one side to avoid actually touching Gere's knees but remained aware of the warmth of his silk-and-wool-clad legs a scant inch away from hers.

A tuxedoed waiter approached almost immediately with a wine list for Gere. Gere examined it, then turned solicitously to Shelley. "Do you have a particular favorite?"

A particular favorite? She always ordered the house wine at Angelo's. "Some—" she started in a squeaky voice, then, after clearing her throat, tried again. "Something . . .white?"

Gere nodded, consulted the list again, then rattled off something impressive-sounding in German to the waiter, who did everything but click his heels together and snap, *"Jawohl!"* before retrieving the wine list from Gere and striding off to fetch the bottle Gere had selected.

Scarcely had he disappeared when another waiter brought their dinner menus. Shelley hesitated, staring momentarily at the crest of the restaurant stamped in gold on the leather binder before opening hers.

It was only natural to be curious about how much this evening was setting Gere back, but the menu provided no such information. There were no prices next to the descriptions of the choices available! She noticed, for the first time, that the menu she'd been given was white, while the one Gere was perusing was royal blue, and much larger. She swallowed the lump that suddenly clogged her throat. How expensive would food have to be that women had to be protected from the shock of seeing the prices?

Although she was flattered that he would bring her to a place like this and probably spend as much money as she made in a week to impress her, she was sorely tempted to lean across the table and say, "This isn't necessary. I'd much rather go somewhere less formal."

Telling herself she was being ridiculous, she drew in a deep breath and forced herself to concentrate on reading the menu. She was here; she might as well enjoy it. *When in Rome—*

In Rome, she would have ordered spaghetti at some sidewalk *ristorante* in typical American-tourist tradition. At Gaspard's, she was forced to choose from a plethora of temptations that ranged from fresh *mahi-mahi* à la Gaspard, to medallions of veal with peppercorn sauce. She decided to bat her eyelashes helplessly and insist that Gere decide for her—unless, of course, he selected the calamari, which even a rural mail carrier knew was squid.

Gere appeared quite comfortable with being charged with ordering for them, and settled on the *mahi-mahi* entrée, preceded by fresh fruit compote and a Caesar salad.

Like a finely-tuned robot, the wine steward appeared with their wine, just seconds after the waiter had taken their order—without writing anything down, Shelley noticed, impressed. She'd spent one summer waiting tables at Denney's, and she could appreciate the mental skill required to memorize orders. Of course, Gaspard's didn't have the turnover that Denney's did during the lunch hour.

The steward made a theatrical production of opening the wine and pouring a finger of it for Gere's approval. Again, Gere—shy, reclusive Gere—handled the situation with a comfortable aplomb. He sniffed the wine, swirled it in the goblet, commented on its bouquet, then sipped, and praised its flavor.

The steward filled Shelley's glass, then Gere's, before coaxing the bottle back down into the ice and discreetly retreating. Shelley was debating whether she was supposed to be the first to drink, until Gere raised his glass in a toast. "To the mail, and the pretty woman who brings it."

Smiling at the flattery, Shelley lifted her goblet to clink it with his. Gere eyed her interestedly over the rim of his own glass. "Good?" he asked.

"Very," she said, sincerely. "It tastes like...sunshine."

"The amount of sun during the growing season influences the sugar content of the grapes, which influences the fermentation process after the grapes are harvested. So, in a sense, part of what you're tasting *is* sunshine."

Shelley studied him over the rim of her glass as she took another draft. He was such a riddle. When she least expected it, he proved to be disarmingly charming. How could a man say love was a luxury of moving up the evolutionary ladder one minute and explain that wine tastes of sunshine the next?

Even his appearance was eerily chameleonlike, with sharp contrasts. Could this man in the sleek, dark suit and silk tie be the man in the tattered Harvard T-shirt and ragtag denim cutoffs who'd signed for the first certified letter she'd delivered to his house? His hair, shaggy when she first met him, then shorn but still unruly, was slicked back and controlled with something stiff and shiny. The severe style emphasized his strong features and, though elegant, was more like that of a gangster or a gambler than a scientist.

"What made you—?"

"What made you—?"

They spoke at the same time, then laughed self-consciously.

"You first," Shelley said.

"I was wondering what made you decide to become a mail carrier."

Shelley lifted her shoulders in a subtle shrug. "It pays well. I get to meet lots of people. And mail's important. I like feeling that I'm doing something significant." She grinned. "Besides, I'd tried practically everything else."

"Like what?"

"I was a waitress. And a salesclerk. Then I worked in an office, answering phones and opening mail and typing address labels. That was okay, but my boss was a grabber, and I was tired of fighting him off, so I started looking around for something else. My best friend, Maggie, was working as a sub—her uncle's a mail carrier and helped her get the job—so I decided to give it a try."

"What's a sub?"

"Substitute carrier. The mail is delivered six days a week, and the regular route carriers just work five. So everyone has a substitute for the sixth day. The subs also take overflow work and new routes that don't have assigned carriers yet, so usually they work a lot more than one day a week. With automation cutting jobs, Maggie and I were lucky to get on when we did."

"What are they automating at the post office?"

"Almost everything. Did you know they have machines that read addresses? Even addresses that people have handwritten. That's pretty amazing, when you consider what some people's handwriting looks like. It's everything I can do to read some of the addresses I see."

"Do you see every piece of mail on your route?" Though Gere managed to sound nonchalant, his discomfort over the idea was evident.

"All the mail for my route comes to me in a big bin. I have to sort it for delivery."

"That must prove interesting," he said tautly.

"Sometimes," she admitted. "But the mail's confidential, so I try not to see anything but the address."

"You don't always succeed, though," he said shrewdly.

The specter of Dr. Hunk was there with them, as imposing as a physical presence. Shelley decided it was time to deal with him once and for all. "Some things are hard not to notice—like mail addressed to Dr. Hunk."

He exhaled a sigh, almost relieved to have the issue finally brought out in the open. "I figured as much. Shelley, those letters—"

She was about to tell him that he didn't have to explain, when all conversation was cut off by the arrival of the waiter with their salad—or, at least, with a cart and everything needed for the preparation of Caesar salad. The waiter's performance was every bit as flamboyant as the wine steward's had been with the uncorking of the wine. With a cleaver, he halved a clove of garlic and then danced the cut edge around the inside surface of a large wooden bowl before putting in the lettuce that had been prepared in the kitchen.

Next, he broke an egg into a bowl and beat it ferociously with a wire whip before drizzling it over the lettuce. With matched silver forks, he tossed the greens until the only visible remnant of the egg was a glossy sheen that clung to the leaves.

He held up croutons, asking for Gere's pleasure. Gere turned to Shelley with an eyebrow cocked in inquiry. Smiling, she nodded, and Gere gave the waiter a similar nod. This elaborate approval process was repeated with crumbled blue cheese, but when the waiter opened a glass decanter of anchovies and Gere turned to Shelley, she wrinkled her nose and shook her head. Gere grinned and shook his head at the waiter, who returned the decanter to the cart with an air of insulted dignity.

For the first time since entering the restaurant, Shelley was enjoying herself. She was aware of being the center of attention as other diners watched the waiter go through his routine and, surprisingly, she didn't mind. Maybe the evening wasn't going to be such a disaster, after all.

The waiter squeezed juice from an cheesecloth-wrapped lemon half into a shaker of oil, then capped the shaker and shook it with a flourish. Finally he dumped the blended dressing over the salad before giving his masterpiece the final, formal toss.

He heaped the fruits of his culinary effort onto chilled plates and set them before Shelley and Gere. Then, with the dramatic gesturing of a magician creating an illusion, he produced a pepper grinder of gleaming dark wood from the bottom shelf of the cart. He wielded the tall instrument with the mien of a samurai with a sword, and asked superciliously, "Would *madame* care for fresh pepper?"

"Please," Shelley said, as the business end of the grinder hovered just inches beneath her nose. She flashed Gere a smile as the waiter made far too much of a production of twisting the top of the grinder. Without warning, Shelley's nose suddenly began to burn, as though she were breathing pure fire.

Before she could identify the reflexive reaction and suppress it, she sneezed. Heartily. Mightily. Loudly enough, she was certain, for every one of the understatedly elegant patrons in that elegant, expensive restaurant to hear. The waiter snatched the pepper grinder away as though he feared she might have contaminated it with enough germs to spark a global epidemic of the Black Plague.

Gere's *"Gesundheit!"* scarcely registered with Shelley as the waiter repossessed her salad plate and said, managing to make the words sound as though they'd slid down his nose, "You'll want a fresh salad. I'll fetch a plate from the kitchen."

Shelley's face—to Gere—was the most imminently watchable face he'd ever had the privilege of beholding. During the most ordinary of moments, it captivated him; during extraordinary moments, it fascinated him.

Because of the emotions that played on those lovely features, this was an extraordinary moment. He watched them register: the horror of humiliation, the denial of what had happened, guilt, and, finally, embarrassment. "No!" she told the waiter, cheeks flushing. "That's not— You don't have to— I don't need—"

"Shelley," Gere said, in a tone of voice so authoritative that it drew her shocked gaze to his. "It's all right. There's plenty of salad left in the bowl. He'll bring a new plate."

The waiter retreated, carrying her plate with the disdain of an orderly for a soiled bedpan.

Shelley's gaze was still locked with Gere's. "I'm sorry," she said meekly.

A touch of color still lingered becomingly in her cheeks. Gere had never worried that the sheer beauty of a woman's blush might stop his heart or paralyze his lungs. But then, Gere had never truly been in love. And he *was* in love with Shelley Peters; hopelessly, totally, irreversibly in love. He couldn't have denied it, even if

he'd wanted to—which he didn't. He was too en-
thralled by the feeling to consider denying it.

"There's no disgrace in sneezing," he said, hoping to
soothe her.

"I've never been allergic to pepper before."

"It was probably a gourmet variety," he explained.
"Fresher than the peppercorns you'd buy at the super-
market."

"I wish I could just disappear into thin air," she said.

"Please, don't. The waiter might make me eat all the
salad, and I wouldn't have room for the *mahi-mahi*."

The witty remark earned him a smile. "Your sister
was wrong," she said. "You have a fine sense of humor."

"She only said that because I don't always appreciate *her* sense of humor. For instance, I wasn't amused
by the ad she put in some lonely hearts column asking
women to write to Dr. Hunk."

"So, that's the story. I suspected it was an ad, because the letters came from all over."

"You thought *I'd* placed it?"

"I didn't know. How could I? But once I'd met you,
it didn't seem like the type of thing you'd do."

It didn't seem like the type of thing you'd do. Suddenly Gere felt exposed. Was her intuition so strong
that she had known he would never presume to assign
such a preposterous name for himself? Did she think
him ineffectual, incapable of anything as creative as
placing a classified ad? Did she think it farfetched that
he might be addressed as Dr. Hunk?

He contemplated the matter as the waiter filled a
fresh plate with salad and set it in front of Shelley. He'd
brought a pepper grinder, also, and his manner was almost offensively condescending as he held it up and

asked, contemptuously, "Would *madame* care for fresh pepper?"

The man's pomposity suddenly threw the entire incident into perspective for Shelley. In the same icy, clipped tone he'd used with her, she replied, "*Madame* would *not* care for fresh pepper, thank you very much."

The waiter nodded curtly to Gere, stuck his nose in the air and departed, hovering over the cart possessively as he wheeled it away.

Shelley reached for her fork but, sensing Gere's attention, rested her hand lightly on the table instead. A glance told her that her intuition had been on target. He *was* staring at her. "I'm sorry," she said. "I didn't mean to lose my temper, but he was so—"

"Overbearing and insufferably rude," Gere finished wryly. "And you handled him beautifully."

His approving smile gave her a warm feeling all over. She wondered why she'd never noticed before that he had a truly remarkable smile, then realized he hadn't done a lot of smiling during their harried meetings at his mailbox. He was different tonight; still shy, still quiet-mannered, but also calmly self-confident. She hadn't thought of him as a particularly large man, but in the VW earlier, and now at the intimate table for two, he seemed physically bigger than he'd seemed in the unconfined space of his yard.

Shelly was aware of him now as a man—a male presence with superior strength. Sharing the small table with him, she could feel the warmth his body generated, and smell the woodsy scent of his after-shave. It was nice, very masculine. She tried to remember if she'd ever noticed the scent before, and decided that she had not. He probably didn't wear after-shave unless he was going out.

Piano music—something mellow and slow—floated in from an adjoining dining room to soften the companionable silence between them as they ate their salads.

"Kevin thinks you have the neatest job in the world," Shelley said, when the waiter had cleared their salad plates and their entrée had not yet arrived. "He was impressed when I told him you studied bugs, but when he found out you had frogs, too, he decided he wants to be an entomologist. I told him he'd have to study a lot."

"And what did he say to that?" Gere asked.

"He said he didn't think he'd mind studying if he could study bugs instead of geography."

"Your brother's very special to you, isn't he?" He could hear the affection in her voice when she talked about him.

"Yes," she replied, and smiled. "I was almost a teenager when he was born, so I've watched him grow up." She took a sip of wine. "He's very bright. He wanted to know what you study about the bugs. I tried to tell him about the chemicals, but I'm afraid I couldn't explain it as well as you."

"I'll bet you explained it beautifully."

"As much as I understood."

"Most people don't even try to understand what I do."

"But you're so passionate about your work."

Gere nearly choked on the wine he'd just sipped. "Passionate?"

"Of course. You believe in what you're doing. Most people just have jobs, but you're trying to do something that will make the world better."

He studied her face intently. "You make me sound . . . heroic."

"Maybe you are," she said.

Gere shook his head, rejecting that possibility. He'd never felt the least bit heroic in his entire life.

"Why not? Most people would like to do something to change the world, but very few are qualified to actually make a difference. You are."

He knew she wasn't actively trying to flatter him, but his ego was soaring, nonetheless. He was human enough to want to hear more. "Qualified in what way?"

She seemed surprised that he would have to ask. "You know how," she said. "You're a scientist."

He laughed aloud.

"What's funny about that?" she asked.

"Nothing. It's just . . . your naiveté is so charming, Shelley."

"I was serious," she replied.

"I know," he said, a smile remaining in his eyes as his gaze met hers. "And your confidence is touching. It's just that true scientific discovery is as much luck as knowledge. Sometimes progress is made inch by painful inch, one step at a time, piling one bit of information on another until it all comes together. But some of the most significant advances in the history of science have been made by pure accident. I could spend the rest of my life looking for useful naturally-occurring chemicals and never find a single one with any practical application."

"Or you could find something that helps millions of people."

"It's a craps shoot, at best."

"Not if you believe you'll find something."

"I appreciate your vote of confidence, Shelley, but it's not that simple."

"Have you tried visualization techniques?"

"Visualization techniques?"

"You've never heard of visualization?"

"Afraid not."

"It's... Well, it's imagining yourself successful so that your mind believes that it's possible."

"You don't really believe that imagining something could make it happen?" he asked, sounding incredulous. The entire concept was contrary to every scientific tenet he believed in.

"It's a matter of opening your mind and allowing events to happen," she explained. "If your mind is closed, you could be staring a discovery in the face and not see it because you're not expecting to find it."

"And imagining it would make it happen?"

"Well, there are no guarantees, of course," she said defensively, irritated by his wholesale rejection of the idea. "It's not magic. You don't just close your eyes and order a dream the way you'd order a sandwich at a deli. But it can't hurt to open your mind to possibility."

She could see the skepticism on his face and argued, "Your mind doesn't know the difference between what you tell it and what really happens. If you're constantly telling it that you won't discover something unless you get lucky, it won't be receptive."

"Did you come up with this ... *theory* all by yourself?"

"No!" she exclaimed, surprised that he would think her capable of it. "Of course not. Lots of people use creative imagery. Athletes use it for a competitive edge, and corporations send their executives to learn the techniques. The class I took was full of salesmen."

"You took a class in imagining?"

"Creative visualization," she corrected. "And yes, I took a class. I take lots of classes. Some people get degrees. I just take classes in whatever I'm interested in." Her forehead crinkled in concentration. "I guess that sounds frivolous to someone with a Ph.D."

Gere shrugged. "It sounds like a pragmatic approach to education." It occurred to him that Kelsey would like Shelley. The thought pleased him.

Between their *mahi-mahi* and dessert, Shelley said, "I could teach you the basics of visualization—how to relax, and how to create an image of yourself succeeding."

Gere grinned. "I think I'll stick to four-leaf clovers and rabbit's feet."

Shelley lifted an eyebrow. "Oh. I see. The scientific approach."

Gere was saved from having to respond by the timely arrival of the dessert cart. Shelley's eyes widened as she beheld Gaspard's renowned desserts: tortes topped with glazed fruit, parfait glasses layered with chocolate mousse and liqueur-laced custard, sliced fruit waiting to be dolloped with freshly whipped cream, and plump strawberries dipped in chocolate.

When she peeled her gaze from the cart to look at Gere and exclaimed, "Oh, my God!" Gere laughed aloud.

"I take it *madame* cares for dessert?" the waiter asked dourly.

"I believe you're correct," Gere answered.

They listened to the waiter's long-winded, glowing descriptions of each of the desserts. After detailing each liqueur, each cream, each type of chocolate, he stepped back and glared at Gere expectantly.

Smiling, Gere cocked an eyebrow questioningly at Shelley, who told him what she wanted.

"One strawberry?" Gere and the waiter parroted in unison.

"One perfect strawberry—'dipped in the finest Belgian chocolate,'" she said, quoting part of the waiter's description.

"The standard order is three," the waiter informed her.

"I just want one."

"You heard the lady," Gere said. "One perfect strawberry dipped in the finest Belgian chocolate." He winked at the waiter. "I'll have the other two."

Later, as they waited in the canopied entrance for the valet to fetch Gere's car, Gere turned to Shelley and asked, "Why just one strawberry?"

"Why a single red rose?" she replied flamboyantly. "Because it was perfect."

But later, in the car, she said softly, "Gere?"

Gere chanced a glance at her. "Yes?"

"About the strawberry."

She spoke with the gravity of a woman about to reveal a dreadful secret, piquing both Gere's curiosity and his concern. "What about the strawberry?" he asked.

"I ordered one because I knew it would irritate the hell out of the waiter." She swallowed, and added gently, "You weren't . . . embarrassed, were you?"

After a beat of stunned silence, Gere burst out laughing. "Embarrassed? I was proud of you! That waiter was a piece of work. I don't know why restaurants tolerate that kind of arrogance, but it seems endemic to the better restaurants."

"I wouldn't know," Shelley said, and instantly regretted the revealing slip.

A long silence followed.

Gere had sensed an undercurrent of discomfort all evening. "Gaspard's was not the restaurant you would have chosen, is it?"

"It was very nice," she said. "The food was excellent."

"Some of my former professors came down last year to tour the institute, and Sondra—my partner—arranged dinner at Gaspard's. Naturally, it was the first restaurant that came to mind."

"I didn't know you had a partner," Shelley said.

Gere was already mentally flogging himself over blowing his choice of restaurant; he didn't want to get drawn into a discussion of Sondra. "I don't have one anymore," he said.

From the tone of his voice, Shelley surmised that his partnership with the unseen Sondra had ended on less-than-ideal terms. The fact that she was a closed subject left Shelley rabidly curious. Had this Sondra been a scientist, too? Had Gere known her at Harvard?

Shelley wasn't jealous, but she didn't like the feeling of coming in a poor second to his mystery partner. Sondra probably hadn't had to borrow a dress to wear to Gaspard's. She probably wasn't allergic to freshly ground pepper, either!

Gere drew her out of her reverie when he said, "I'm not a very social person. I don't go out very often, so I'm not adept at planning—"

Shelley put her hand on his forearm to soothe him. "Gere, I enjoyed going to Gaspard's. Really. I'd heard a lot about it, but I'd never been there."

"You probably go out all the time."

"I don't sit around the house much," she admitted.

"Where do you go with your friends? What do you do on Saturday night?"

"Whatever seems right at the time. Dinner. Movies. The usual."

Gere considered her answer a moment, then asked, "Is there anything you'd like to do tonight?"

"Tonight?"

"It's still early," he said. "If there's something—"

Shelley could tell from the way he threw out the invitation that it was important to him that she come up with a suggestion. Frantically she considered possibilities. There was a movie she'd been wanting to see, but, while it was only ten, by the time they bought a newspaper and found out where it was playing, it would be too late to catch a showing. And she couldn't imagine playing volleyball at the Beachcomber's Club in her Pilgrim dress. There was always Angelo's, but it would be crowded by now. They needed a quiet place where they could talk and become better acquainted.

She pointed at the roof of the car. "Does this top go down?"

"Yes. Sure."

"Then what are we doing with it up on a beautiful night like this?"

Gere lowered the top, then turned to Shelley, who had switched on the radio and was searching for a station. "Where to?"

"One of my favorite places," she replied, leaning back in the seat and looking at the stars. "Just keep driving until I tell you to turn."

Fifteen minutes later, following her directions, Gere pulled the VW into a small park. The parking area faced a little lake, still and indigo-black except for the reflected moonlight that danced on the surface.

"What do you think of my lake?" Shelley asked.

"It's lovely," Gere said, but he was more interested in Shelley than in the moonlit water. Water and moonlight he could have any time he cared to hike out to the pond at the back of his property—this was his first opportunity to feast on Shelley in the moonlight.

She seemed almost to glow in the pale light. Her hair—its curls seeming to capture slivers of moonbeams and bend them into gentle arcs—surrounded her face like a golden halo. Her face was all highlight and shadow, her skin translucent and bisquelike.

Even with the background of soft rock on the station she had tuned in, he could hear the soft whisper of air inhaled and exhaled as she breathed.

"This is great," she said. "I'm so used to being in the Jeep with both doors open that I feel kind of closed in in most cars." She turned to look at him, and smiled. "I don't have any problem adjusting to convertibles, though."

Resting her head against the seat back again, she closed her eyes, took a deep breath and released it as a sigh. "This place is unbelievably peaceful at night."

Did she know what she was doing to him? Was she doing it on purpose? That sigh. The way she was tilting her head back, exposing her neck. He could feel her breathing as he watched the subtle rise and fall of her chest; it took his own breath away.

"Do you come here often?" he asked.

She opened her eyes. "Not as often as I'd like. I wouldn't want to be out here alone at night." Her voice changed to a wry, teasing tone. "The maniac with the hook might get me."

She seemed to assume he would know what she was referring to. He didn't. "Maniac with the hook?"

"You've never heard about the maniac with the hook?"

He shook his head helplessly.

"You must not have gone to many slumber parties when you were growing up."

"No," he confirmed. "Not many." *In fact, none.* He'd camped some as a student, doing fieldwork, but he'd never been to the kind of sit-around-the-campfire-and-tell-spooky-stories kind of slumber party she was talking about. "Tell me about him."

She took the storytelling tone he assumed she might use with her younger brother—or with a roomful of giggly little girls preparing to be scared out of their wits. "One night, on a night very like this one, a boy and a girl, very much like us, went to a park, very much like this one. They were talking and listening to the radio, and smooching. . . ."

She paused to let the significance of that sink in before continuing. "Suddenly, the announcer broke in over the radio with a special bulletin. You see, an inmate of a local asylum for the criminally insane had escaped, and he was believed to be wandering in the area. Instead of a right hand, he had a hook, and he'd used it to torture people, so he was considered very dangerous."

Gere was fascinated, both by the story and by her relish in telling it.

"Well," she continued, "the girl was scared, and she wanted to leave, but the boy. . . Well, he was kind of enjoying the smooching. . . ."

"Hmm," Gere said.

"So he didn't want to leave. Well, they argued a while, but the girl *insisted*, so the boy finally relented and peeled out in a huff. And all the way home, they kept hearing this funny little clunk-clunk sound against the car door, and they couldn't figure out what it was until they got to the girl's house and the boy opened his door so he could go around and open the girl's door for her. And do you know what it was?"

"I have a terrible sinking feeling that I do," Gere replied.

"That's right! It was a hook, closed around the door handle. And the next day they found out that the maniac had killed four people at that very same lake." She waited for him to comment. He didn't. "It's supposed to be a true story."

Gere's "Humph!" carried a lot of skepticism.

"Feel like a stroll in the moonlight?" she asked. "There's a hiking path around the lake."

"Aren't you afraid we'll run into the maniac with the hook?"

"I'll take my chances," Shelley said. "Besides, I have a big, strong man to protect me."

Gere savored the idea of being cast in the role of her protector, even in a hypothetical situation, against an imagined antagonist. "Let's live dangerously," he said, reaching for the door handle.

The path wound along the shore, leading them past clusters of ducks sleeping with their feathers puffed out and their heads tucked under their wings. Every so often, a sudden breeze tweaked the water, temporarily turning the moon's reflection into a turbulent, undulating swirl of butter yellow and sending the usually lazy water slapping against the shore.

One of the sleeping ducks roused as they approached, lifted her beak, regarded Gere and Shelley hopefully; then, seeing that the humans had no food to offer, she tucked her bill back under her wing and fluffed out her feathers again, as if to tell them she was sorry she'd wasted her time.

"I think we've just been snubbed," Shelley said with a chuckle.

"First the waiters, and now the ducks," Gere added drolly.

Suddenly, spying a playground off to the left, Shelley broke into a run, calling over her shoulder, "Bet I can swing higher than you can!"

It was the last thing in the world he would have expected her to do when she was dressed oh-so-properly in that chaste black dress. Dazed by the situation, Gere chased after her and settled into the swing next to the one she had chosen. Shelley had already pushed off, working up momentum by the time Gere got used to the feel of the flexible rubber seat hugging his backside, and launched into flight with a shove of his foot against the ground.

Shelley pumped her legs furiously, urging her swing higher, and Gere followed suit. He hadn't been in a swing since childhood, and he'd forgotten the feeling of absolute freedom, the soaring sensation of flight on the upward climb and free-fall on the backward stroke.

As if she'd read his thoughts, Shelley said, "This is almost as great as a convertible."

"Better," Gere said, as her swing passed his on an upstroke, and her outstretched leg sliced into his field of vision. Her skirt billowed and rippled in the wind, waving proudly as a flag.

How long they went on swinging, he couldn't have said; he knew only that although it should have been all wrong—the timing, their ages, the way they were dressed—it was peculiarly right to be there swinging alongside her, at night, in their dressy clothes.

Just as she had been the first to run to the swing, Shelley was the first to slow down, coasting to a gentle sway. Gere stopped his swing with his foot. "Tired?"

Shelley took a deep breath and released it slowly. "No. Just ready to try something new."

"What now?"

"Adventure," she said, getting out of the swing. She waited until he'd done the same, then led him to the heart of the playground, where a grouping of wooden structures stood isolated and motionless like giant animals hunkered down for the night. "We didn't have playgrounds like this when I was little," she said wistfully. "It was just plain old merry-go-rounds and seesaws."

She regarded the various structures carefully, then took off for a wood-and-rope monstrosity at one corner. Tentatively stepping onto a wood-plank bridge with rope sides, she said, "I went through here with my brother once. It makes you feel totally out of control."

The heel of her shoe lodged between two of the planks, so that when she raised her foot to take another step, her foot slid out. "This was easier in sneakers," she said good-naturedly. She knelt to pick up the shoe, and took the other off as well, then dropped them both over the edge. "Remind me to get those before I leave."

Progress on the unsteady bridge was slow. It swayed and jiggled with their every movement, forcing them to cling to the rope handrail as they inched along, and Gere's heavier weight pulling behind her kept her in an uphill struggle. One misstep sent the entire bridge into a frantic gyration, and she fell back against Gere. "You don't have to be a child to do this, but it helps," Shelley said, tugging her way back up the rope.

"Interesting sensation, having the ground shift beneath your feet." He wasn't referring to the bridge; the ground beneath his feet had shifted the instant Shelley's shoulder had lunged into his chest.

Shelley tugged her way back up the rope. "Kevin shimmied up this thing like a monkey going up a tree."

"What's at the top?"

"Wait and see," Shelley replied.

It took them another two or three minutes to reach the top, where the ladder and the rope handrails fed into a large, woven-rope pen with a floor similar to the safety nets used by trapeze artists. With a whoop of delight, Shelley made a flying leap for the center of the net. It lurched under her weight. She lost her balance, and plopped into a sitting position, legs apart, her skirt spread around her like a rag doll's.

Rushing to see if she was hurt, Gere lost his footing on the unstable netting and pitched forward, knocking Shelley back, landing with his arm across Shelley's waist and his nose pressed against that pristine white collar of her dress—smack-dab between her breasts.

Mortified, he arched away. The abrupt movement set the net into wavelike motion. He struggled vainly for some purchase on the jiggling surface, but the net sagged under his weight, and gravity delivered a giggling Shelley to him on a roll. Having encountered an immovable object at the lowest dip of the net, she put a hand on Gere's chest to steady herself.

Such a simple gesture, that hand on his chest. She placed it there so easily, so casually, without a trace of self-consciousness. But Gere's reaction was anything but casual. He felt the warmth and weight of every one of her fingers, just as he felt the pressure of her breast against his ribs and her hip against his thigh.

"It's like swimming in gelatin," she said delightedly.

More like drowning in sensation, Gere thought, wondering if she was even vaguely affected by the closeness dizzying him.

Cradled in net that flexed around them, urging them together, they remained still until, eventually, the fitful convulsions of the net slowed, seguing into a gentle sway. The net became a giant hammock for two under a canopy of clouds and stars surrounding a sliver of moon. Gentle gusts of wind whispered through the treetops, an occasional bird called in the distance, crickets chirped from their grassy hideaways.

Shelley sighed a languid sigh that tiptoed over Gere's nerve endings like a centipede in ballet shoes. "I can't believe how peaceful it is here," she said.

"Heaven," Gere agreed. He'd have sacrificed a year's research work to make love to her there, under the stars, but he didn't know how to ask, and he was too afraid of blundering to risk a mistake.

"When I was a child, I used to watch the clouds for hours, deciding what they looked like." She pointed. "That one's a rabbit."

Gere considered the cloud thoughtfully, then said, "Looks like a wasp to me."

"That's the magic of cloud watching. You see the things that mean something to you. I see a rabbit because I like cuddly little bunnies, and you see a wasp because you like wasps."

"What if you don't find anything you like?"

"Then all you have to do is wait, and the wind will draw something new for you. See? The rabbit's turning into a heart."

"The wasp's turning into a honey bee," Gere disputed wryly.

Shelley didn't argue the point with him. It was too mellow a moment for debate. After a long stretch of silence, she said, "This would be a good place to try imaging."

"Imaging?" It was so far from what he'd been thinking that Gere had to shift gears in his mind. "Oh, yes. Imagining your way to success."

"Everyone said I was crazy to hope to get on as a mail carrier at twenty-two, but I imagined myself in the Jeep, delivering mail, and before long, I got on as a substitute."

"And the rest, as they say, is history," Gere finished, obviously dubious.

"Come on, give it a try," she said. "It can't hurt."

Gere wanted to remain in her good graces. "What do I do?"

"Start by relaxing."

Easy for you to say, Gere thought. His desire for her was coiled inside him like a tightly-compressed spring, and the deep breath she took to demonstrate the relaxation process only wound the spring tighter.

"Go on. Pick a star to focus on and take a deep breath."

Gere made a halfhearted attempt.

"You're so tense," Shelley observed. "This training would be good for you, help you relax. Have you picked out a star? Show me which one you're focusing on."

Gere chose one at random and pointed. "That one."

"Good. Now, concentrate. Breathe deeply. Try not to think about anything but your breathing and the star."

Concentrate on a star when he had Shelley Peters's warm body alongside his? When her breast moved against his ribs each time she filled her lungs with air? She had to be kidding!

"Pretend that your body is hollow and someone is pouring warm wax into you, and as the warm wax flows down inside you, you relax, and get heavy, and sink farther into the net," Shelley instructed.

Gere was still, almost unnaturally still. "Do you feel yourself getting heavy?" Shelley asked.

"You could say that," Gere answered lethargically.

"Good. Don't fight it. Just let yourself get heavier and heavier." She'd begun to wonder if he was going to co-operate at all, but if anyone she'd ever met needed to learn to loosen up and dream a little, it was Dr. Garrick Booth. "Close your eyes when your eyelids get heavy."

She closed hers, and waited a moment. "Do you have your eyes closed?"

"Umm."

Shelley took that for a yes. "Now think about something you'd like to discover, and see yourself finding it, like you're looking in a mirror while you work, or watching a tape of yourself. Concentrate on what it is you want, and see yourself doing it."

She took another deep breath. "Can you imag—?"

The question was swallowed by a kiss as Gere's
mouth fused over hers. At first Shelley was too surprised to move, but gradually the gentleness of the kiss
permeated her senses, seducing a response. Though his
mouth was gentle on hers, their full-body embrace was
devastatingly intimate. The sagging net seemed to be
pressing them together from all angles, making the
contact more intense than if they were standing. Gere
was practically on top of her, his body heavy and hard
and hot with arousal.

Shelley gasped at the strength of her own response,
parting her lips as she slid her arms around him, wondering how anything so unexpected could feel so incredibly right. She had thought he might want to kiss
her good-night. She had thought she would keep it
short and sweet and chaste. She had thought their relationship would be more platonic than romantic.

*She must have had rocks in her head to think such
thoughts!* Platonic? From her rushing pulse to her tin-
gling toes, every fiber in her body mocked the idea of
a platonic relationship with the man kissing her.

Such a kiss could surely melt stone! His mouth was
gentle yet insistent, his lips soft and sensual as they
moved persuasively over hers. His hands touched her
with reverence—firm, yet caressing; strong, yet care-
ful not to abuse strength; questing, yet not greedy. His
touch—the arousing sweep of his fingertips on her face,
neck and waist—tantalized and bewitched, yet did not
violate.

After lifting his head to end the kiss, Gere continued
holding her, and looked down into her face, his eyes
glowing warmly with reflected moonlight. Shelley
waited, wondering if he was going to speak. It seemed

to her that the kiss had ended all too soon—and its effects were lingering far too long.

"You were supposed to be concentrating on something you wanted very badly," she said tremulously.

Gere chortled devilishly. "I was."

6

FLATTERY. SHELLEY HAD never realized how deadly potent it could be. Tacked onto that gentle, reverent kiss, it was even more devastating. She felt as though she might liquify at any moment and seep through the holes in the net supporting her.

She raised her hands to his face, resting her fingertips lightly on his cheeks, and met his warm gaze. It was like peering directly into his soul. She saw both his desire for her, and his vulnerability. Still cradling his face, she lifted her head until her lips touched his briefly, then lowered her head and smiled.

They lay on the net for a long while, silent, aware of each other, savoring the night and their nearness, until a flicker of light in the copse of trees at the playground's edge caught Shelley's attention. She pushed up on one elbow, still watching, until she saw another flicker. "Lightning bugs! The first ones I've seen in years!" She turned to Gere. "What makes them glow like that? I've always wondered."

"It's oxygen reacting with luciferins—substances stored in their fatty tissues."

"Do they have any control over it?"

"Absolutely. Their nervous system stimulates the air tubes that carry the oxygen."

"Does it feel good?"

"Feel good?"

"When they glow."

"I don't know."

"I think it must. Otherwise, why would they send the message to the air tubes to send the oxygen to the . . . lucifer-whatevers?"

"Luciferins," Gere said, and grinned. "And they light up because they're lonely. It's their means of finding other lightning bugs."

"When they want to mate?"

"Yes."

She giggled. "That's a new one. Get horny and shine."

Gere stared at her for so long that she wondered if he disapproved of her bluntness, but he allayed that fear with a benign chuckle. "You have a refreshing way of looking at things. Sometimes it's good for scientists to hear a nonscientific perspective."

"My perspective is about as nonscientific as a perspective gets. It's interesting, though, how and why insects do the things they do."

"Actually, lightning bugs are a bit unusual, not only because they have the capacity to produce light, but because they are one of the few nocturnal insects that use sight to locate each other. Most use scent."

"They *smell* each other?" Shelley asked incredulously.

"Yes. Moths in particular produce chemical attractants called pheromones."

"Who produces them—the males, or the females?"

"Both. The female releases a pheromone that lures males."

"Like perfume?"

Gere laughed. "A little. That's a good analogy, except that moths produce their attractants internally instead of getting them out of a bottle. Anyway, when a male moth smells the female's pheromone, he flies to her and releases his own pheromone to see if the female is receptive."

"If she did her thing to attract him, doesn't that mean she's interested?"

"Not always. The females tend to be very selective."

"Hunks only, huh?"

Gere flashed her a wry grin. "We're just beginning to find out what makes the females accept or reject a potential mate. There's some evidence that the diet of some male moths enables them to produce chemicals that repel predator insects, and that a female is more interested in those males. She instinctively selects the male who offers the best chance of survival for her offspring."

Shelley was pensive a moment, then asked, "And the female moth can tell this by smelling his pheromone?"

"Observation suggests that she can."

"How convenient."

"Convenient?"

"Sure. All she has to do is smell his pheromone to know if he'd be a good father. It's a lot more complicated for human beings."

"Life is considerably more complex for human beings than for insects. Most insects have a life span of less than a year. They hatch, they mature, they mate, they reproduce and they die. Their entire existence is instinct-based, and most of their actions are fixed and inchangeable. Human beings, on the other hand, live longer and, so long as their basic needs are being met, have intellectual agendas."

"Intellectual agendas, huh?"

Gere nodded.

"Too bad that doesn't necessarily make them smart."

"You don't think human beings are smart?"

"Not necessarily," she replied. "Especially when it comes to picking out mates. The chemistry that draws people together has nothing to do with what kind of people they are, or what kind of parents they'd make. People are just as likely to fall for someone who's totally wrong for them as they are to fall for someone who's right."

"Are you speaking from personal experience?" He tried to make it sound casual and light, but he was anxious to hear her answer.

"No," she said thoughtfully. "I've been pretty lucky, and I'm just naturally kind of cautious about relationships. But I have plenty of friends who would have appreciated some kind of 'sniff test' to help them weed out the turkeys before they got involved in a bad-news situation. My best friend would love it if jerks emitted some kind of 'jerk alert' stench."

"Negative pheromone," Gere mused. "Interesting concept."

"The real jerks would probably find a way to mask it," Shelley said. And then, after a thoughtful pause, she added, "You know, if a woman did what a female moth does, she'd be considered a gold digger."

"How's that?"

"If she selects a husband based on what a man has to offer her children, then she's more or less marrying for money instead of love, and most people would say that's mercenary."

Gere considered the idea for a moment. "That's a relatively new perception in our culture. Throughout history, men have sought women who could produce healthy heirs, and women have sought mates who could protect and provide for them and their children.

In ancient times, it was the best hunters, because they could keep the family supplied with furs and skins and food."

"And nowadays, it would be the man with the most money, except that women are supposed to be too independent to notice anymore, which is a hoot, because women still don't make as much money as men, and they still take most of the responsibility for the children and household," Shelley said. She plopped back onto the netting, looking up at the sky. "I think I'll become an insect. Life would be much simpler."

"Much shorter, as well," Gere pointed out. "One life cycle."

"If we were insects, we could just stay here under the stars all night long."

"That's a powerful argument." Gere settled beside her. "I'm not going anywhere, are you?"

Shelley cuddled closer, tucking her forehead against his arm. Obligingly, Gere extended his arm, offering her his shoulder for a pillow.

"Hmm." She sighed. *Was there anything more comforting than a man's shoulder? A man's strength curled around you?*

She felt she really could stay there all night with Gere—and might.

The perfect moment was abruptly shattered by a blinding beam of light from below. "All right, you two. Get on down."

Gere leaped into a sitting position and peered down through the net. "What the—?"

Shelley felt him tense. Her eyes adapted to the light enough to distinguish the form of the man holding the huge flashlight—and a county sheriff's deputy's uniform. The officer was middle-aged, a bit paunchy, and looked as tough as his voice was gruff. His right hand hovered over a holster holding a gun about ten miles long and as big around as a telephone pole.

"You two get down from there. I want to see some identification."

Gere gave Shelley a look he hoped was reassuring before replying, "We're not harming anything, officer. We were just sitting here looking at the stars."

The officer harrumphed grumpily. "It's obvious what you two were doing, otherwise I'd have my weapon drawn. But the playground closes at sundown, which makes you trespassers. Now get down here, and let's see that identification."

"It'll take us a while," Gere said, remembering the ascent on the rope ladder.

"I hope you're not planning on packing a picnic basket before you get started," the cop retorted sarcastically.

"We're on our way," Gere said, shrugging at Shelley.

With gravity on their side, going down was considerably easier than going up had been. In less than two minutes they were standing in front of the cop, while the officer studied their driver's licenses under the beam of his flashlight. Much to their relief, he had holstered his gun.

"Are we under arrest?" Gere asked, mentally evaluating the effect of negative publicity on the institute's reputation if news of an arrest hit the papers.

The cop raised the beam of light to Gere's face. "You drive here?"

Gere nodded.

"What kind of vehicle you driving?"

"Volkswagen. Bug convertible."

The cop lowered the flashlight and handed Gere his driver's license. "Glad to hear it. I found it on my rounds. The engine was still warm, but nobody was around. I didn't know whether to have it towed, or send out a search party."

"All's well that ends well?" Shelley interjected hopefully.

The cop thrust her license under his light, then raised the beam to her face. Satisfied that her face matched the photo, he returned her license and switched off the flashlight, then turned to Gere. "You two are a little old for this kind of foolishness, aren't you?"

"There's no such thing as too old when you're with a woman who looks like Miss Peters," Gere said, grinning wickedly.

The cop gave Shelley a once-over. "I can't argue with you on that one, mister."

"Doctor," Shelley corrected, and both men gaped at her in surprise. "He's a doctor," she told the cop defiantly. "He has a Ph.D. From Harvard."

"Is that so?"

Gere nodded. "Two, actually."

"Well, for an educated man, you're not being very smart, putting a nice girl like this in danger," the cop said. "You know what goes on in this world today. There's a weirdo around every corner. You two were so caught up in each other, you didn't even hear me walk up. You're just lucky it was me who came up on you, and not some maniac."

One look. One look at Gere's face was all it took. The cop had inadvertently used the wrong word. "It could have been the maniac with the hook," Shelley whispered, and after a beat of charged silence during which they fought for control, they burst into laughter.

"You two been taking drugs?" the cop asked, snapping to alertness.

"No, sir," Gere managed to get out between guffaws. "It was just . . . a private joke."

Gere managed to attain some semblance of a straight face, but lost it when Shelley looked at him again and burst out with a fresh giggle.

The cop shook his head and muttered,

"Saturday nights. You know, kiddies, I've got drunk drivers to chase down. I don't need to be baby-sitting a couple of overgrown teenagers. If you'll lead the way to your car, I'll take a look at the registration papers, and we can all be on our merry way."

A few minutes later, they exited the park, Gere turning the Volkswagen one way onto the highway, the deputy turning his cruiser in the opposite direction.

"There go our tax dollars at work," Shelley said, twisting to watch the cruiser's taillights disappear in the distance. She settled back in her seat. "I thought I'd collapse when he said he could have been a maniac."

"It was a rare moment," Gere agreed. "He had a point, though. We didn't hear him walk up. We'd have been sitting ducks for any vagrant or derelict who happened along."

"We should have checked the netting for hooks. The cop may have scared off the maniac in the nick of time."

Gere didn't adopt her teasing tone. "He implied that I blithely put you in a dangerous situation, Shelley. I would never do that intentionally."

"Hey—the playground was my idea, remember? I just didn't know we were going to get kicked out by a cop with an attitude."

"You're not . . . offended, then?"

"Offended?" She laughed off the possibility. "It was priceless! That cop has clearly worked one too many crime scenes."

The radio was still on the nostalgic rock station she'd tuned in earlier, and "St. James Infirmary" was playing. "I love this song," Shelley said. "My sister used to have the single. It was an oldie even when she was a teenager, but it one of her favorite songs to dance to. It's sad, but the melody's beautiful."

She grew very still, listening to the haunting tune. When it was over, she said, "What you told the cop tonight, about never being too old when you're with a woman like me—that was a sweet thing to say."

"I meant it."

"I know." *That's what makes it so sweet.* "I'll tell you one thing, Dr. Booth, no one's ever going to accuse you of taking a girl on an ordinary date!"

"But I want to!" he said intensely. Unexpectedly, he guided the car onto the shoulder of the road and stopped. He turned toward Shelley as far as the bucket seat of the car would allow and studied her face a moment before raising his hand to slide his forefinger over the graceful curve of her cheek, then forward, to trace her lips. He poised his own lips as if to speak, but released a shuddering sigh instead. "It's so clear in my mind what I need to say to you. Then I look at you, or smell your perfume, and suddenly everything is all muddled."

He propped his elbow on the back of her seat, and though he wasn't actually touching her, Shelley was heartily aware of his physical presence. He wasn't the only one who fell victim to occasional muddle-mindedness.

"Shelley, when it comes to women—" He rammed his fingers through his hair—or tried to. Encountering a crust of hardened styling gel, he muttered something vague about a damned sticky mess and dropped his hand into his lap. He took a deep breath and started over. "The truth is, I don't know the first thing about women or dating. It's like I'm in an alien land, and don't know the customs."

Shelley rested her hand on his forearm. "You've been doing just fine. You were right at home at Gaspard's."

"But you weren't, and that's my point. I know we're different, Shelley. Our lives are different. I'm—I know people think I'm weird, living out there by myself studying bugs. I've just never had a reason to want to change anything. Until now."

His gaze was piercing as his eyes met her. Shelley could feel his intensity; she tasted it on the roof of her mouth as she swallowed. Her voice came out raspy and tight. "Gere—"

"I want to know you, Shelley. I want to know everything about you. I want to take you somewhere where you feel at home, and see what your life is like."

He wiped his hand over his face. "I must sound obsessed."

"A little," she admitted meekly.

"Maybe I am," he said grimly, and started the car. Neither of them spoke again until they were standing on the narrow landing in front of Shelley's front door. Shelley unlocked her door and opened it, and then they looked at each other, each at a loss over how to break through the awkwardness that had developed between them.

Finally, Shelley stood on tiptoe and kissed Gere's cheek. "It was a lovely evening. Thank you."

Gere recognized the overly polite, scripted quality of the statement and panicked. The evening was ending, and she was about to disappear behind that open door, and instinct—his only guide at this point—told him that if he let her go with nothing but a rote, good-mannered "Good-night," he'd never see her again except sitting in her Jeep stuffing mail into his mailbox.

He grabbed her hand, capturing it in his own larger one. She didn't try to pull away, which he took as an encouraging sign. "It's not an unhealthy obsession," he said. "I'm not dangerous. It's just that . . . you fascinate me."

He didn't know how to interpret her quiet smile, or the brightness in her eyes that looked like potential tears. He decided the brightness was a trick of the moonlight, because there was no earthly reason he could think of that she might want to cry.

So he focused on the smile, and took courage from it. "I want to see you again."

Her eyes were brighter than ever, her confusion and uncertainty obvious.

"Give me a glimpse of your life," he pressed, as she hesitated.

"One of the mail carriers is giving a sort of birthday party for her husband next Saturday out at Pleasure Island. There's a group going. I could use an escort."

"I would be honored," Gere said, grinning like an absolute fool.

"I NEED HELP."

"Hello, Gere. It's so nice to hear from you. How's the weather down south?"

"Cut the sarcasm, Kelsey. I'm desperate. I have a date."

"So you got up the nerve to ask her. Great!"

"*Another* date," Gere said. "We went out last night."

"Good for you! How'd it go?"

"Go? It went *splendidly*. Shelley's allergic to pepper."

"Well, I know if I were a man, that'd be the first thing I'd look for in a woman."

"You don't understand. She was . . . splendid."

"Must be the word for the day."

"You're always nagging me to go out. I thought you'd be happy for me."

"I am. I am. Now tell me, what did she do that was so splendid?"

"She sneezed on the salad and ordered one strawberry for dessert. I thought the waiter was going to pop a stud on his pleated shirt."

"That's nice, Gere. So, you went somewhere really nice. Did you get . . . you know, romantic?"

He chuckled lecherously. "Yes."

"Gawd, Gere, I can hear you drooling through the phone line. Just how romantic did you get?"

"Very. Plenty romantic. I was doing great until the cop showed up."

"Cop? Gere? *A cop?*"

"The playground was closed."

"You were in a *playground?*"

"It was . . . phenomenal, once we made it up the rope ladder. I'm thinking of buying a hammock for the backyard."

"I don't think I'm old enough to hear any more."

A silence ensued. When Gere finally spoke, he was very serious. "I need help, Kelsey. This time we're going out with her friends."

"So?"

"So? This is *important*, Kelsey. I can't make a fool of myself."

"You're not going to make a fool of yourself. Relax. Last night went okay, didn't it?"

"Last night I got by with a dark suit and a white shirt, and the playground just...happened. Next week they're going to a place called Pleasure Island. I did some checking. It's part of the Disney complex. A night spot."

"You can handle it."

"It's a party spot, Kelsey. They have a New Year's celebration every night. All the clubs have dancing."

"So?"

"*Dancing*, Kelsey — I don't know how to dance."

"So? You're a genius. Learn how."

"In six days?"

"All you need is a box step for the slow dances. You can fake your way through the fast stuff."

"Is that all?"

"Piece of cake! Just go to the library and check out a how-to video. It's about time you used that VCR of yours for something besides looking at magnified bugs."

"They actually have tapes that show you how to dance?"

"They have videos that show you how to give birth, how to clean and fry catfish and how to make bird feeders from milk cartons. Of course they have videos that show you how to dance! Have you got a pen and paper handy?"

"Hmm? Oh, sure."

"I'm going to give you the titles of some movies to watch for the fast dances. Let's see—there's *Saturday Night Fever, Dirty Dancing*—'"

Gere laughed. *"Dirty Dancing?"*

"Where have you been in the last century?" Kelsey asked, sounding anguished. "Oh, and be sure to get a movie called *Footloose*. Kevin Bacon actually teaches another character to dance. You can fast-forward through to that scene and watch it as many times as you need to."

"You really think I can pull it off?"

"I know it, Gere. They'll play ten fast songs for every slow song. All you'll have to do is move in time with the music. It'll probably be so crowded you won't have to move much. In fact, the music will be so loud that you won't even have to talk."

"What do I wear?"

"Since when do you care about clothes?"

"I have to make a good impression," Gere said intensely.

There was silence on Kelsey's end of the line, then, "Oh, Gere. You've fallen head over heels with this girl after one date, haven't you?"

"I thought you wanted me to find someone special."

"I do, Gere, but haven't you ever heard of taking things slowly? You should sample a variety of fruit before you decide what kind of tree to plant. What do you know about this girl?"

"I know I'd like to have a tree."

"You thought the same thing about Sondra."

"Leave Sondra out of this. Shelley's nothing like her."

"That doesn't mean she won't break your heart, when you insist on wearing it on your sleeve. As much as I hate playing the devil's advocate here, Gere, you and Sondra had a lot in common, including your work."

"You couldn't stand Sondra!"

"No. I never liked her. She was too ambitious. I knew she was going to break your heart. And I was right. I just can't stand the thought of you rushing into another situation. What do you have in common with this girl?"

"Butt out, Kelsey." His voice had an edge.

"Take it slow, huh? Cut loose and have some fun, but keep it light. I mean, what could you possibly know about her after one date?"

"She—" His mind crowded with images and memories. Of Shelley's smile. Of the warmth in her voice when she talked about her little brother. Of the way she felt, snuggled up against him. But words failed him.

"She could be after your money, Gere."

"Now you're being ridiculous. She doesn't even know about the trust fund."

"Maybe not. But she's seen your land, and your house, and she knows you're director of the institute. Two hundred thousand would look pretty good to a woman who makes twenty thousand dollars a year, even if she didn't know about the millions."

There was a awkward silence, then a sigh swished through the phone line. "I know whereof I speak on this."

Gere knew Kelsey was sincere in her concern. He knew she was hurting, the way she always hurt when she remembered the fortune hunter who'd deceived and seduced her, then broken her heart when she was naive and vulnerable. But he couldn't let her indict Shelley. "Don't condemn a woman you've never met because of your bad experience," he said.

Kelsey was quiet—too quiet—for a long time. Then she said, softly, "I just don't want to see you hurt again, Gere."

"Then quit mother henning me and tell me what to wear! I've got a woman I want to impress."

"It's about time!" Kelsey said. And, after a pregnant pause, she turned serious. "You know, Gere, clothes, hair—they're just externals. You're a good person. That's what's going to shine through in the end."

"Yeah. Right. Everybody loves a nerd."

"You're no nerd, Gere. You're just a diamond in the rough."

They fell silent. Finally Kelsey said, tentatively, "Gere?"

"Hmm?"

"You'll be responsible, won't you? I mean . . . safe?"

Gere was certain his face was ten shades of purple.

"Kelsey!"

"Sorry, I've been working on my sex-ed lectures for my health classes."

"Would you quit treating me like one of your wet-behind-the-ears students just because I need some fashion advice. I watch the news, you know."

"Sorry, Gere." She switched back to their original subject. "So, Dr. Hunk, have you considered getting some new glasses?"

"I just got new glasses."

"Didn't you say they were identical to your old glasses?"

"My *good* old glasses, not the old, old broken ones."

"Didn't you say that you had to special order them from the factory because the local optical shop doesn't stock them anymore?"

"Yes. So what?"

"Doesn't the fact that they were discontinued tell you anything, Gere?"

"The optical shop has no class?"

"You've got your favorite glasses to wear every day. Get yourself a pair for social occasions. Look for the word *designer*. They'll be expensive, but splurge. Gold wire rims in an interesting shape would look great on you."

"You've been wanting to tell me that for years, haven't you?"

"You turkey! I *have* been telling you that for years. You've just never paid any attention. You must *really* like this woman."

Gere let his silence speak volumes.

"I don't suppose you'd consider an earring," Kelsey suggested hopefully. "You'd only have to have one ear pierced, and it doesn't hurt but a second. Honest."

"I'd sooner eat a live earthworm," Gere replied.

There were limits to what he would do—even for Shelley Peters.

"Well, then," Kelsey continued with renewed enthusiasm. "Ready to take notes? Let's start with the pants."

SHELLEY DROPPED gratefully into a molded-plastic chair at one of the plastic tables in the food court at the mall. "Shopping has got to be as exhausting as long-distance running."

"Yan-n-ck!" Maggie said, imitating a penalty buzzer. "Nice try, but that excuse does not justify the calories in those chocolate-chip cookies you just bought."

"To hell with calories, I need energy!" Shelley insisted, taking one of the cookies out of the bag. "It's hard work finding just the right thing for a man who's turning thirty. But I think we hit the jackpot with the 'vitamins.'" The gag gift was shaped like a huge pill bottle and filled with candy-coated chocolate candies, with Geriatric Vitamins spelled out on the fake prescription label in large letters.

Maggie removed the lids from the lemonade they'd bought to go with the cookies and set one of the cups in front of Shelley. "I liked the book better."

"Well, who wouldn't be thrilled to get his own copy of *Thirty and Smart's Better Than Twenty and Dumb as a Doorknob?*" Shelley agreed drolly.

Maggie took a sip of her lemonade, then sighed. "I hate shopping for people I don't know all that well. You don't think Stan's going to be offended, do you?"

"From what Barbara says about Stanley, he's incapable of being offended. Besides, once he opens the present Barbara got him, these'll look tame."

Maggie reached into Shelley's cookie bag and snitched half a cookie. "What'd she get him?"

"You didn't hear about it? She had them at work yesterday, showing them around. She got him a pair of leopard-print bikini underpants with a red satin heart over the crotch that says, Thirty And Still Down And Dirty."

"He's going to die."

"Are you kidding? You've met Barbara's husband. They don't call him Wild Stanley for nothing."

"You're right. He'll wear them to work and drop his pants to show the secretaries."

"Do Barbara and the secretaries a favor and don't suggest it, okay?"

"What does Barbara see in him?"

"Love is blind," Shelley said, digging for the lemon wedge in her glass with her straw. "Besides, he's not so bad. He's just . . . Wild Stanley. He's a little immature, and a little uncouth, but he's crazy about Barbara."

"And vice versa," Maggie added, and heaved a heavy sigh. "Wild or not, at least he can make a commitment."

"So tell me about your blind date," Shelley urged. "How bad *was* your sister-in-law's cooking this time?"

"My brother grilled steaks," Maggie said.

"And your date?" Shelley prompted, cocking an eyebrow.

"You know how it is," Maggie said. "There were ... my sister-in-law, my brother, Roger's mother and father, *Roger....* It was awkward for a minute, but we got past it."

"So, what was he like?"

Maggie shrugged. "Fair to middling. His parents moved here last year, and Roger just finished his degree at the University of Missouri and came down to see if he'd like to live here."

"You must have liked him a little bit, if you invited him to Pleasure Island tonight," Shelley pointed out.

"You've heard of marriages of convenience? This is a date of convenience. Sort of a mutual mercy date. I needed a date and he doesn't know a soul in town, and I think he was glad to have an excuse to get out of his parents' house for a few hours."

"You didn't like him at all?" Shelley asked sympathetically.

"He didn't set off any skyrockets." Maggie sighed. "He seems nice enough, but what do *I* know? You know my track record—another Saturday night, another jerk."

"Maybe it'll work out."

"Maybe. And even if it doesn't, I won't be the only one at the party without a date, and he won't be watching television with his parents Saturday night."

Shelley pinned Maggie with a shrewd look. "It's that time of the month again, isn't it?"

"Does it show?"

"Some women turn into witches. You get morose."

"You're my best friend. Cheer me up!"

"Sorry. I'm fresh out of knock-knock jokes."

"Then depress me. Tell me about you and Dr. Hunk."

"It won't depress you," Shelley said.

"Oh, yes, it will—because it's you instead of me. And I can tell from that lovesick grin on your face that it's going to be beautiful."

The grin blossomed into a full-blown smile. "It shows?"

"Hey, this is Maggie, your best friend, remember? You've managed to avoid talking all week, but now I want details."

"He's different from any man I've ever known," Shelley said. "He was so—" She finished the statement with a sigh.

Maggie frowned. "You can't leave that hanging. Some of us have to live vicariously. He's so *what?*"

"It's hard to describe. Polite. Gallant. Attentive. Intense. *Nice.*"

"You've sold me. Box him up. I'll take him."

"Over the corpse of our friendship," Shelley said.

Maggie looked surprised. "It's that serious?"

"It could be," Shelley admitted.

"I told you you were weird about this guy. Last week you weren't even sure you weren't going out on a mercy date and this week you're waltzing a foot off the ground when you talk about him. What happened, Shel?"

Shelley looked her best friend dead in the eye. "He kissed me."

IT WAS THE ARMS—what was he supposed to do with his arms? Realizing he had to have help, Gere sauntered from his den to the kitchen. "Mrs. Northbrook?"

His housekeeper stopped her mopping and stood at full height, throwing her shoulders back much like an army private in the presence of a general. "Dr. Booth?"

Gere swallowed, feeling foolish and self-conscious. "Mrs. Northbrook, do you know how to dance?"

"Dance?" Laugh wrinkles framed her eyes as she gave him an indulgent smile. "Well, I haven't mastered the lambada, but I've cut more than a few rugs in my day."

"I'm trying to learn the box step."

"Well, good for you. Who's teaching you?"

"I am. I mean, I'm trying to teach myself. I checked out a video, and I think I've mastered the step, but it's difficult to tell without a partner. Would you mind—?"

Mrs. Northbrook laughed, propped the mop handle against the counter, and self-consciously wiped the palms of her hands against her denim skirt. "The last thing I expected today was an invitation to dance. At least my feet won't get sore." She lifted her right foot and rotated her ankle, showing off the thick-soled nurse-type shoes she was wearing. "Of course, you realize, I smell like pine cleaner."

"That's all right," Gere said. "I really hadn't noticed." How could he not notice the pungent odor of pine cleaner in his own kitchen when he never failed to notice the scent of Shelley's hair spray from a distance of ten feet?

"Oh. You've got the furniture moved back and everything," Mrs. Northbrook observed, following him into the den.

Gere blushed. "I've been practicing. I had some videos, and I've been trying to follow along. I think I've learned the pattern of the steps, but—"

Mrs. Northbrook gave him a look she'd probably perfected on her grown sons. "Well, as the song says, it takes two to tango."

It took only seconds to work out the positioning of hands, and start moving to the music. "You've got the steps down, but you've got to loosen up," Mrs. Northbrook told him.

Gere was concentrating too intently on his footwork to reply.

"I knew something was up when I heard the music," Mrs. Northbrook continued.

"The music?" Gere echoed, finding conversation distracting.

Mrs. Northbrook nodded. "Umm. You're usually playing classical." She tilted her head back so she could see his face. "How is it that an educated man like you never learned to dance?"

"It wasn't a required course," was the most accurate answer he could think of.

"You must have a new lady friend," Mrs. Northbrook speculated.

"Yes."

"Good for you. Is she pretty?"

Gere remembered Shelley's face in the moonlight. In the candlelight of the restaurant. In the sunshine when she delivered the mail. He thought of her smile, her eyes, the graceful slope of her neck and shoulders. Of her legs, bare and beautiful in the shorts she wore to work, stockinged and svelte when she wore that black dress. "Yes," he replied. "She's quite pretty."

"I thought she must be. You're going to an awful lot of trouble to impress her." A couple of minutes later she said, "You're doing real good, Dr. Booth."

"It *is* easier to practice with a partner."

"It'll be easier with your lady," Mrs. Northbrook said. "Just wait—once you put your arms around her, you won't even have to think about your feet. You'll just float."

They danced through another couple of songs before Mrs. Northbrook patted him on the arm maternally. "You've got the hang of it now."

"I hope so," Gere said, exhaling a weary sigh.

Mrs. Northbrook patted his shoulder. "Just wait. You'll see. She'll think you've been dancing since your diaper days!"

Placing her fists on her waist, she eyed the heavy leather sofa and armchairs he'd shoved up against the wall. "If you'll leave this room like this, I'll vacuum in here before I go. I like to get under everything at least a couple of times a year, but your furniture's too heavy for me to move around."

"You should have said something," Gere told her. "Any time you need it moved—"

"I was getting primed up to ask." She shrugged her shoulders. "Well, I'd better get back to that kitchen floor before I have to start over from scratch."

Gere stopped her as she was leaving the room. "Mrs. Northbrook?"

She turned, lifting an eyebrow.

"Thank you," he said.

She dismissed his gratitude with a wave of her hand. "My pleasure, Dr. Booth. And don't you worry about a thing. When you get all gussied up in your weekend duds and get that pretty little girl in your arms, dancing will feel like the most natural thing in the world."

"I hope so," Gere muttered under his breath. "I sincerely hope so." But as fervently as he hoped he would magically float across a dance floor, he was apprehensive about his upcoming date. His apprehension continued to escalate as Saturday night approached.

When, finally, he stood in front of the mirror in his bathroom evaluating the sum of his efforts, he was both pleased and skeptical. He looked the part he was trying to play: fashionable, macho, hip. He'd gone to the flashy unisex salon in the mall and let a buxom stylist trim and comb his hair for him. He'd bought the cotton pants with pleats Kelsey had told him to buy. A very solicitous salesgirl had obligingly rolled up the long sleeves of his striped overshirt for him, and helped him pick out the perfect knit muscle shirt to go under it. He'd even spent an alarming sum of money on a pair of shoes that reminded him of those worn by Frankenstein's monster.

But, beneath the externals, he still *felt* like Gere Booth, a social black sheep disguised in party wolf's clothing, an imposter destined to be exposed. A man could dress like a clown, but when he opened his mouth and croaked like a frog, the world would find out he wasn't the lead singer from *I Pagliacci*.

It had been a week of study and shopping. If not for his daily meetings with Shelley at his mailbox—brief, chaste encounters rife with knowing smiles and sexual tension and the promise of sweet things to come—he might have abandoned his quest for social acceptance, but those daily doses of Shelley reminded him why it was important to prove he could fit into society.

Still, doubts nagged at him as he drove to her house. Trying to impress a woman was one thing, but when it reached the point where he felt he was trying to be something or someone he wasn't, it was beyond simply trying to make a good impression. It was trying to make a false impression. Who did he think he was, anyway—Dr. Hunk?

He fumed at his own folly as he walked up the short walk to her front door, and fumed some more as he waited for her to answer his knock.

Then she opened the door.

7

"GERE," SHE GREETED, smiling broadly as she gave him a once-over. "You look . . . great."

Gere wished she didn't sound quite so surprised. Or delighted. Studying the laces of his high-top basketball shoes, he muttered, "Thanks." He forced his gaze back to her face and grinned self-consciously. "I couldn't take a woman dancing in my tromping-around-in-the-bushes clothes."

"You cut your hair again," Shelley said, amazed at the transformation. Shorter on the sides and spiked on top, it was still stiff, but a great improvement over the rather severe mafioso look of the week before.

"You look nice," he said, knowing that her shirt—what there was of it—was going to torment him. The soft yellow knit molded her breasts and was held together between those twin peaks by a row of tiny buttons. As if to deliberately tantalize, the top four buttons were left open, and the sides fell apart haphazardly, forming a soft V that revealed just enough cleavage to hold a man's eyes hostage. The hem of the shirt reached exactly to the top of the waistband of the ruffled denim miniskirt, threatening to provide a glimpse of skin as she walked ahead of him to his car.

She crossed her legs as she settled into the passenger seat, and Gere remained achingly aware of how exposed they were. While actually no shorter than the shorts she usually wore on her route, the miniskirt nevertheless seemed less substantial. The stretch of exposed thigh between her knee and the bottom ruffle of denim seemed longer than mere inches, and the knowledge that a man could follow that luscious thigh with his hand and eventually encounter lacy underwear was enough to set Gere's teeth on edge as he drove to the restaurant where they were to meet her friends.

The restaurant was in a commercial plaza still crowded with shoppers. "This isn't a valet kind of place, I'm afraid," Shelley said, as Gere drove up and down several long rows of automobiles in search of an available parking space.

"I don't mind walking," Gere assured her, then, with a stricken look, offered, "I could let you off at the door so you don't have to."

"I don't mind the walk," Shelley replied, and smiled. "Besides, I'm going to be the envy of every woman in the place when I walk in on your arm."

"*Under* his arm" would have been a more accurate description of how she entered the restaurant. She fit there perfectly, her shoulder nestling naturally and cozily in the juncture of his arm and torso as he extended his arm across her shoulders. She was conscious of him next to her—his male warmth and male hardness, the fragrance of his after-shave.

She hadn't made the comment about envious women simply to flatter Gere. Somewhere, somehow, at some point in time, he had metamorphosed from a nerdy mad scientist into a hunk. Female heads were, indeed, turning—discreetly in some cases, blatantly in others. Maggie, and even happily married Barbara, turned a bit giddy when Shelley made the introductions, and more than once Maggie cast her astonished looks of inquiry and near-comical lifts of eyebrow when no one else was looking. Shelley almost dreaded the inevitable inquisition the first time Maggie got her alone.

The ax fell when the women retired to the ladies' room while the men worked out the check. The door had scarcely closed behind them before Barbara and Maggie both assaulted her with questions.

"Where did you find that man you're with?" Barbara asked. "He's scrumptious."

"She found him on her route," Maggie said, crossing her arms in front of her waist and fixing Shelley with a you'd-better-explain-yourself-quick glare. "What gives, Shelley? You said Dr. Hunk was anything but a hunk!"

"I told you he bought some new clothes," Shelley said defensively.

"Clothes don't make *that* man, Shelley," Barbara opined.

"She's right," Maggie said. "And you let me think you were going out on *mercy* dates!"

"I never said he was ugly."

"Well, you never mentioned that he was the most delicious man to come along since Rhett Butler carried Scarlett O'Hara up the stairs, either."

Shelley sighed. "I'm as surprised as you are. Everything about him's different. His clothes, his haircut, even his glasses." *But not his smile. Not the warmth in his eyes. Not his passion. Not his basic goodness. Not any of the things that make him the person he is.*

"We could all live with that kind of surprise," Maggie said wryly.

"Roger seems nice," Shelley commented, deliberately changing the focus of the conversation. "Anything heating up between you two?"

"Not a chance," Maggie replied. "It's strictly friendship. He has a girlfriend."

Surprised, Shelly turned away from the mirror to look at Maggie. "A girlfriend, as in serious?"

Maggie frowned. "He told me in the car on the way here. She's got another semester of school, and they haven't told either of their parents about their relationship because they don't want to play Twenty Questions, so he couldn't tell me Thursday night in front of his mother. If he's found a job by the time she graduates, she's moving down here. Otherwise, they're both moving to St. Louis, where she's from. My luck . . ."

"At least he told you up front," Barbara pointed out.

"Yeah," Maggie said bitterly. "He's a real up-front guy all right. I finally find a man who can make a commitment, and he's already made it to someone else."

"They can't all be hunks," Shelley taunted affectionately.

Maggie stuck out her tongue playfully. "Sure, Shelley. Rub it in, rub it in."

"Stan seemed to enjoy his presents," Shelley remarked.

"Stanley loves anything that makes him the center of attention," Barbara said. "He's in hog's heaven every birthday."

"I was worried about how Gere would take it—you know, being with total strangers, and the crazy gag gifts and everything. He's so shy . . . but he handled it well, didn't he?"

"I would never have suspected he was shy," Barbara agreed. "That crack he made about the 'well-dressed perverts' was pretty funny."

"He's a genius," Maggie said. "Harvard."

"He really captured Stan's attention with that stuff about ordering ladybugs to control aphids on his rosebushes," Barbara said. "The idea's just oddball enough to spark Stan's imagination, especially if he can be the first one in the subdivision to try it."

"It's not an oddball idea," Shelley countered. "It's just progressive. Gere's concerned about the environment. He's devoting his life to finding ways to preserve it."

Barbara paused in the middle of applying a fresh coat of mascara to eye Shelley curiously. "You're really hung up on him, aren't you?"

"She's weird about him," Maggie said. "She always has been."

"It's easy to see why," Barbara said, and resumed putting on her mascara.

Shelley took a long look at Barbara's reflection in the mirror. *She doesn't see anything,* she thought. *All she sees is a hunk. She doesn't see the person he is at all—only the clothes he's wearing, and the way he combed his hair. And neither did Maggie.*

And less than a month ago, neither had she. The realization saddened her. She was not a shallow person, yet she'd been ready to make a snap judgment about Gere, based solely on appearances—just as her friends had done. She didn't consider Barbara and Maggie shallow, either. No woman who could see past Wild Stanley's brashness and pomposity and love him could be considered shallow, and Maggie, for all her cynicism about men, had a soft spot in her heart for misfits and underdogs.

No, they weren't shallow, not any of them; not shallow, just ready to accept everything at face value because that was the most expeditious way to pass judgments and form opinions. If Gere hadn't given her those beetles for Kevin's lizard, she might never have probed the depths of his eyes, might never have accepted a date with him, might never have gotten to know him for the remarkable person he was. She wouldn't have been with him up on that net canopy under the stars, would never have kissed him....

AT THE PLEASURE ISLAND ticket office, Shelley and Maggie flipped out annual passes. Gere and the others bought one-night tickets, and they all entered the park through the turnstiles, where attendants stamped their hands. Stages, neon-lit club entrances, vending carts and lighted display windows lined streets filled shoulder-to-shoulder with people determined to have a good time.

Except for the occasional tourist family, the crowd was predominantly couples on dates, old enough to drink but young enough for their nervous systems to tolerate the cacophony of music belched from loudspeakers and performers on the various stages. The atmosphere could only be described as controlled mayhem.

Before deciding what to do first, they made a circuit of the park, checking which clubs had lines waiting to get in and which were less crowded. They stopped to watch an athletic young man wearing a Velcro jumpsuit fling himself against a Velcro wall, trying to land in ever-more-bizarre positions.

Gere observed the peculiar phenomenon with a gnawing sense of dread. Kelsey had told him to be a good sport and participate in any activity going on. Did that mean he should take a turn in the Velcro suit? He waited to see how Stanley handled the situation. "Wild Stanley," Shelley had called him. Surely if Wild Stanley didn't volunteer, most likely a mild-mannered entomologist wouldn't be expected to.

Much to Gere's relief, Wild Stanley lost interest in the acrobatic show after only a few minutes and wandered to the opposite side of the street, where a muscled stud was trying to impress his date by ringing a "thermometer" bell by pounding a lever with a sledgehammer.

Gere was more fascinated by Shelley's reaction to everything than by the spectacles surrounding them. Along with the rest of the crowd, she applauded when the bell rang and the muscle-bound stud claimed a kiss from his date, a striking redhead who willingly obliged.

She has an annual pass. The fact wedged in his logical mind as if driven there by a hammer. How often did she come to this place? Did she thrive on this confusion, this chaos?

Would she kiss him the way the redhead was kissing the muscleman if he rang the bell? Would she kiss him that way if he didn't? What if he tried, and failed—was there a consolation kiss?

He had a sinking sensation that he was about to find out as he noted with trepidation that Wild Stanley was purchasing a ticket to wield the sledgehammer. Whatever Wild Stanley did, Gere Booth would do. He didn't want to risk appearing to be, in Kelsey's words, a "deadhead."

He watched Stanley make a production of weighing the heavy hammer in his hands and then doing a series of slow-motion hammer blows that stopped just short of the hammerhead, hitting the lever that set the clapper in upward motion. Stanley was a rather nondescript man, average in height, ten pounds heavier than he should be, with medium brown hair and animated brown eyes. There was an affability about him that made his unorthodox manners not only tolerable, but appropriate. The nickname of "Wild Stanley" fit, but his wildness was benign.

The clapper climbed two-thirds of the way up the thermometer with Stanley's first blow, higher still on the second, but Stanley refused to give up and paid for a third try. Everyone applauded his determination when the gong rang on his third blow. Stanley clasped his hands together and raised them above his head like a triumphant prizefighter and bowed to the cheering crowd, then flamboyantly exacted his reward kiss from his wife with the plea, "You ought to give me that present now. I earned it."

"You've got all the presents you're going to get until your birthday," Barbara stated firmly. Brown-haired, petite and feminine, Barbara was as down-to-earth as her husband was outrageous.

Wild Stanley turned to the others. "She has this crazy notion about waiting until after midnight, since tomorrow's the actual day." Curling a finger on the ribbed neck of her shirt, he pulled it away from her skin and peeped down inside. "Hard to believe she's hiding something down there."

Slapping away his hand, Barbara said, with an edge in her voice, "Cut it out, Stanley."

Stanley shrugged. "The woman's impossible."

"Next!" called the ticket hawker. "Who's going to impress the little lady?"

Wild Stanley looked at Roger and Gere. "You two going to give it a go?"

"Not me," Roger said. "I just graduated from college. My mind is keen, but my body's out of shape." While he hardly looked like a man who'd gone to seed, he was slight of build and gentle of speech, so his refusal surprised no one.

That left Gere, with Kelsey's imploration echoing in his mind like a litany: *"Don't be a deadhead. Don't be a deadhead. Don't be a deadhead...*.

"I'll give it a try," he said, reaching for his billfold. Then, to Shelley, he added, "Don't expect too much. I haven't been pumping much iron lately."

Shelley couldn't believe Gere was going to try that stupid hammer-bell game. Wild Stanley would have kept shelling out money all night until he finally rang the bell, but that didn't seem like Gere's style at all. She gave Gere an encouraging smile as he tested the weight of the sledgehammer in his hands. His answering smile was courageous if not confident.

Must be some kind of testosterone effect, Shelley thought, a little disappointed that Gere felt compelled to prove his manliness in such a hokey, macho way. *As if she weren't aware of how virile he was!*

Stanley leaned close and spoke into Gere's ear, and Gere nodded gravely, deep in concentration. There was a male camaraderie between them that no woman could breach. Shelley watched with a growing sense of astonishment the seriousness with which Gere was taking the senseless game, and tried to suppress the disappointment she felt. Gere was the last man she'd have expected to indulge in such macho silliness.

All along the meter which ultimately led upward to the bell, there were comic descriptions intended to categorize the strength of the man hitting the lever. Gere gritted his teeth and fervently hoped that he wouldn't miss the lever altogether and, barring that dire fate, that his hammer blow would rank somewhere above "You've got to be kidding!"

Stanley had advised him to hit slightly off center and forward. Gere raised the hammer above his head—no

mean feat in and of itself—and lowered it, guiding it off
center and forward. It was one of those moments when
everything seemed to move in slow motion. He held his
breath and watched the dinger climb up the measure.
Past "Consult A Physician." Past "Weakling." Past
"You've got to be kidding!" Past "Gallant effort." Past
"Nice try." Past "Almost."

Finally, incredibly, the clapper reached the top and
impacted the round bell, producing a crystalline note
that vibrated like a tuning fork. Gere laughed aloud,
more with relief than pride. *Wait until Kelsey heard
about this!*

Then he remembered the tradition of victory kisses,
and forgot all about his sister. He reached for Shelley,
and the next thing he knew, the ticket hawker was tap-
ping him on the shoulder. "Excuse me, sir, but this *is* a
Disney park, and there *are* children in the crowd."

Stunned, Gere searched Shelley's face for signs of the
embarrassment he was feeling, and found only an
impish, mischievous grin. Perplexed, he followed her
gaze to the hawker—a fresh-faced, clean-cut, whole-
some young man whose wry, tongue-in-cheek expression explained everything: The rebuke was all part of
the fun.

Gere heaved a sigh of relief. He hadn't overstepped
the bounds of decency, hadn't humiliated himself and
Shelley, hadn't been creating a spectacle at all. The
young man was simply playing for the crowd. It was
show biz, Disney-style.

Nevertheless, the young man's comment became the
catchphrase and running gag of the evening. Every time
he so much as held Shelley's hand, one of the people
with them would mimic the hawker. "Excuse me, sir,

but this *is* a Disney park, and there *are* children in the crowd."

As the evening progressed, every possible variation was tried: Maggie's Mickey Mouse imitation led to Stanley's Donald Duck; Barbara did an atrocious Bette Davis; Roger tried a less-than-convincing John Wayne, substituting "pilgrim" for "sir."

The twenty minutes they spent in line waiting to be admitted to the comedy club afforded the longest, most quiet interval of opportunity for the friendly harassment. When Wild Stanley tried to top John Wayne by doing Jimmy Cagney with "you dirty rat," and Maggie did a generic tough-girl cop using "scumbags," Gere, frustrated, grumbled to Shelley, "I can't even hold your hand!"

Shelley put her hands on his shoulders. "Don't let them get to you." Then, smiling suggestively, she cooed, "Come on, Doctor Booth, *make my day.*"

Gere ceased caring about anything except Shelley as she slid her arms over his shoulders, and he lowered his face to hers. The next thing he felt, aside from the all-consuming sweetness of sensation that was Shelley, was a tap on the shoulder. He tore his mouth from Shelley's only far enough to mumble, "Buzz off, bug."

"Suit yourself," Stan said. "But we've been waiting almost half an hour for them to open the club, and the line is finally moving inside."

Shelley withdrew her arms from his shoulders but, laughing, grabbed his hand. "Come on. We'll get trampled if we don't move."

The moment Gere had been dreading came when they left the comedy club: They were going dancing. After another lengthy wait, during which Gere grew ever more dreadful of getting on the dance floor where he could conceivably make an absolute fool of himself, they were admitted to a world of flashing lights, dizzying motion and what Gere would forever after think of as a wall of sound. They made their way through a milling crowd, down two flights of stairs, to a circular dance floor that revolved slowly, adding to the perpetual-motion effect. Tables done in a hi tech motif lined the partition surrounding the dance floor, but they were so crowded that there was no hope of getting a seat anytime soon.

The whole place reverberated with the music. Gere felt the beat in his chest the way he might have felt an electronic vibrator, and remembered the movie he'd seen about deaf kids dancing to music they "heard" through vibrating floorboards.

Conversation was out of the question, but no one else seemed to mind. Stanley and Barbara had already taken the leap onto the moving floor, while Roger appeared almost as overwhelmed as Gere felt. Maggie and Shelley were swaying with the beat of the music, obviously ready to dance.

Gere took a moment to study the dancers, and was heartened that what Kelsey had told him was borne out by reality: There was no right or wrong, because every dancer on the floor was doing something different. He'd practiced enough in front of the mirror, aligning his image with the ones in the videos he'd rented, to know that he had mastered basic wiggling well enough to fake his way through the fast songs. He might *feel* like a fool, but he was going to blend in.

He fortified himself with a deep breath, then raised his eyebrows in question and tilted his head toward the dance floor.

"Love to," Shelley mouthed, and led the way. She hadn't been sure Gere would want to dance. He hadn't been a font of enthusiasm when she'd told him about the dance clubs at Pleasure Island. In fact, he'd been so diffident that she'd wondered if he even knew how to dance. Once again, he had surprised her.

Soon after they stepped onto the revolving floor, she realized that people were watching Gere. At first, it was women—not entirely unexpected in light of the way his cotton denims showed off his behind, and the way he'd left the front of his striped shirt open almost to his waist, exposing the teal-blue muscle shirt beneath.

He looks like a stud sent over from central casting, Shelley thought wryly, trying to be pleased with this new aspect of his personality. What girl wouldn't want to be with a man who drew admiring glances from other women? But he didn't just look good. Oh, no. Not the ingenious, full-of-surprises Dr. Hunk. He moved beautifully, too, as though he'd been trained by professional choreographers. And, after a while, it wasn't just women looking at him, admiring his moves and his backside, it was men as well, noticing the effect Gere was having on the women, and grabbing surreptitious looks at the target of their envy.

In a rowdier place, all that macho envy might have created an explosive situation. But for all the noise and the bars, Pleasure Island wasn't the type of place men went to get liquored up and start fights. So the men just looked, fumed and sulked a bit, and danced a little harder to try to outdo Gere, who seemed totally oblivious to all the emotional intrigue revolving around him.

In fact, Gere appeared oblivious to everything except the music . . . and Shelley. She couldn't accuse him of inattentiveness, for despite his fierce concentration on the music, every time she caught his eye and smiled, he returned a smile endearing enough to melt her heart. Eventually she quit worrying about the women drooling over Gere, and their jealous boyfriends, and simply enjoyed being with him, moving seductively to the music, smiling coquettishly, shaking her shoulders and hips a bit more provocatively for Gere's benefit.

After a few songs, they left the floor for a breather, huffing and puffing from exertion—and grinning at each other like adolescents in the throes of a first crush.

Their relationship had reached a new plateau. Shelley's senses thrummed with her awareness of his presence. The kiss they'd shared outside the comedy club bound them now, body and soul. It had been a splendid kiss, freely given, gratefully received, an acknowledgment of the attraction between them, a promise of what could be. She was reminded of that kiss each time he touched her, each time he smiled at her.

"Would you like a drink?" he asked, leaning close to speak into her ear in order to make himself heard above the music.

She gestured toward the bar, where the customers were three deep. "It's not worth the hassle. Aren't you warm?" she asked, touching the rolled-up sleeve of his shirt, which was wilting a bit in the heat, despite starch. "You could take this off, you know."

Gere gave her a puzzled look and cupped his hand over his ear to indicate he couldn't hear.

"Take it off," she repeated, pantomiming sliding the shirt over his shoulders.

He appeared more perplexed than ever, and she boldly grabbed the sides of his shirt near the waistband and yanked it free, then shoved the fronts back

over his shoulders until it hung around his middle,
straining against that one buttoned button.

Shelley pointed, and Gere obligingly unbuttoned it,
astounded at having a woman he desired almost to the
point of insanity undress him—literally—in public. His
imagination embellished, expanded and explored the
possibilities of the situation, and his body tautened in
response. Shelley, seemingly oblivious to the volcano
of sexual energy she was stirring up, captured the
sleeves of his shirt as they slid off his arms and then un-
rolled the sleeves and tied them around Gere's waist,
leaving the tail of the shirt suspended over his hips, the
knot over his belly button and the ends of the sleeves
hanging from the knot. Straightening everything, she
said something that got lost in the din of the music. He
shook his head helplessly.

"Very fashionable!" she shouted near his ear.

Gere shrugged. Fashion was the last thing on his mind
at the moment. Though he was blessedly cooler without the shirt, he was hotter than ever for Shelley. It was
her shirt that was driving him crazy. If he had to undo
buttons, those were the ones he would have preferred
to deal with. In his mind, he'd deepened and widened
that great divide between her shirtfronts a dozen times,
had brushed that yellow knit aside with his fingertips
and tested the smooth texture of her breasts with his
tongue.

He capped her shoulders with his palms and looked
into her face. He'd enjoyed dancing more than he'd allowed himself to hope he would because he'd been
dancing with her, and she'd been dancing *for* him. Now
he longed for more, and wished they were alone—away
from this cursed, pulsating music so that he could wrap

his arms around her and fold her against him and kiss her until the rest of the world lost its meaning.

And then, a miracle happened. The music changed abruptly, to something slow and sensuous.

Perhaps not everyone recognized it as a miracle, but Gere was no fool. He'd wished for the opportunity to pull Shelley into his arms and hold her close, and the sophisticated sound system had finally served it up. He was too delighted to be anxious about whether or not he'd move his feet properly.

By the time he remembered to be concerned, they were already dancing. Floating, as though they'd been dancing together for years. Which probably meant, Gere thought dreamily, that Shelley was an excellent dancer, and he'd gained enough practice with Mrs. Northbrook not to humiliate himself. After making that profound analysis, he quit thinking altogether and surrendered himself to the pleasure of having Shelley Peters in his arms, of having Shelley Peters's cheek resting on his bare shoulder, of being the recipient of tiny nibbling kisses from her clever mouth. He buried his face in her hair, savoring its texture against his cheek, its scent.

She sighed, and the exhaled sigh shuddered hotly over his skin, setting him afire. Was this what dancing was like? Were the other men on this ridiculous twirling floor experiencing the same rich emotional fullness he was? How could they—when he was the only one lucky enough to be dancing with Shelley? Yet they could be feeling something similar, something equivalent.

Gere issued a sigh of his own. The theory certainly explained why dancing was a part of almost every culture known to man. He closed his eyes and focused on the pleasure of being exactly where he was, doing exactly what he was doing. Who was he to buck thousands of years of social custom?

Eventually the mellow song was replaced by another fast one. Gere let go of Shelley, reluctantly giving up the intimacy of the full embrace, then watched her intently as she danced to the earthy beat of the new piece, savoring the memory of how her body had felt pressed to his as they moved together. He accepted the gift of her alluring, enigmatic smile, and wondered how long it would be before he'd be able to wrap his arms around her again.

The next time the revolving floor passed the sideline area where Maggie and Roger had been standing most of the evening, Barbara waved, and pointed to her watch. Gere cupped Shelley's elbow as they stepped off the moving floor.

"It's eleven-thirty!" Barbara shouted above the music. "If we want to see the New Year's show, we ought to get out to the main stage."

The crowd was already thick around the stage, where a live band was playing Caribbean rock. A troop of dancers led the audience in clapping to the frantic beat. A huge countdown clock ticked off the seconds.

"Seventeen minutes to midnight," Shelley said.

"Seventeen minutes till Stanley enters a new decade," Barbara goaded amiably. She had her right elbow looped around his left, and used her left hand to punch him playfully in his upper arm. "How does it feel to be seventeen minutes away from pushing forty?"

"You'll find out next year, won't you?" Stan parried.

Barbara looked ready to come back with another playful retort when they suddenly fell victim to an assault of liquid string. Shelley had to laugh at Gere's reaction when he wiped a glob of the congealing string from his cheek, and stared at the lime-green goop incredulously.

"It's party string," Shelley explained. "It comes in aerosol cans."

"You've got it in your hair," he said, picking at a long strand of it.

"It's all right," Shelley said. "It doesn't—" The word *stick* lodged in her throat as his thumb brushed her cheek and their gazes locked. The raw desire she saw in the depths of his eyes made her swallow. There had been something special about the way he made her feel, from that first kiss at the playground.

Funny how, up until that kiss, she'd thought of him only as a nice person, a friend. As anything except a virile, sexy man who could set off fireworks with a kiss.

Funny how, since that kiss, she was aware of him as a man the whole time she was with him—of his size, his warmth, his strength, his tenderness. When she had lain next to him on that playground net with the stars overhead and he'd surprised her with that kiss, she had felt with him the way she'd been waiting to feel with a man since her storybook days of believing in happily ever after.

Her early boyfriends, with their clumsy kisses and frenzied groping, had shown her the difference between romantic expectation and reality. Then there had been the first great love of her life, the boy to whom she'd surrendered her virginity with complete confidence that he was the man with whom she would build the perfect life—until he'd gone away to college and they'd slowly grown apart.

The next year, when she'd first moved out of her parents' home, she'd had an affair—pleasant, exciting, an adventure. The relationship hadn't ended badly; it had simply ended when she realized it was heading nowhere—that the young man was a good lover, but poor husband material.

The affair had matured her, and her expectations had become more pragmatic. She no longer expected to find a Prince Charming but, rather, hoped to find someone with whom she could, through determined effort and lots of compromise, live with in reasonable harmony for the rest of her life, or his. She had long since lost faith in finding the elusive, magical *zing!*—the instantaneous awareness of sexual chemistry when she looked into a man's eyes, the breathless anticipation of a touch, the heart-stopping thrill when that touch finally came.

And then Gere had kissed her. That single kiss seemed a milestone, a marker, the dividing line between the first part of her life and the rest of her life. It wasn't his haircut that made the difference in him, nor his clothes; not the fact that he'd metamorphosed into a hunk, complete with social graces and hot moves on the dance floor. It was his intensity, his sensitivity, his sincerity; the way he held her as though afraid she might break, then hugged and kissed her as though he might draw the very life from her. Maggie was absolutely right: She *was* weird about Dr. Hunk—when he was a hunk, and even when he wasn't.

Gere diverted his gaze and feigned keen interest in the plastic string he had picked from her hair. "You're right," he said. "It doesn't stick."

He studied it curiously, rolling it between his fingers to test the texture of it, even raising it to his nose to sniff, testing for scent, then looked at Shelley. "You say this comes in aerosol cans?"

It was easy to envision him studying bugs the same way, with an everything-else-be-damned concentration, that brilliant mind of his teeming with details and processing them like a computer. Feeling her heart turn to warm mush, Shelley explained, as if to a curious child, "Yes. It shoots out soft, and hardens when it hits the air."

"Probably a compound with alcohol or some other quickly evaporating liquefier."

"People have it at parties all the time. I'm surprised you haven't seen it before."

"I don't go to many parties," Gere said. *And Shelley had an annual pass to this island of perpetual parties.*

Shelley slid her arms around his waist. "Well, I wouldn't worry about it. You'll probably see enough string tonight to make up for it."

Catching a whiff of her hair—what *was* it she used that smelled like heaven?—Gere ceased to care about string that spewed from aerosol cans. That she should spontaneously wrap her arms around him, hug him...

Lost in his reverie, Gere jumped when a long ribbon of the neon-green substance landed on his ear. Almost instantly, a strip of hot pink settled in Shelley's hair.

Wild Stanley had bought two cans of "string" from a street vendor.

"Stanley!" Barbara warned. "Behave yourself!"

"Oh, lighten up!" Stanley replied amiably. "It's not every day a man turns the big three-oh."

"Thirty going on five and a half!" Barbara countered. "It's only five minutes until midnight—don't you want to save some to celebrate?"

"After midnight I'm going to be too busy admiring my new golf club," Stanley said, pointing the cans skyward and pressing the nozzles. String shot upward several feet, then descended over them in a shower, raining into their hair and over their shoulders.

Laughing, they picked at it, forming it into balls and tossing them at each other as the music grew louder and more frantic than ever, and the crowd thicker and noisier. String flew in all directions, while people clapped, gyrating with the music, counting down the seconds of the last half-minute. The din became deafening, the press of the crowd stifling—not that Shelley or Gere minded being forced into intimate contact. At midnight cannons boomed, spewing confetti that hung in the air like a flurry of snowflakes in a blizzard, landing in their hair and clinging to the folds in their clothing.

The performers marched off the stage and started a conga line that grew as the revelers latched on and snaked its way through the less involved onlookers. Overhead, fireworks exploded into huge balls of flashing glitter.

"I can't believe they do this every night," Gere shouted, brushing confetti from his shoulders.

"Every night is New Year's Eve," Shelley quoted from the television commercials. She studied Gere's face for several seconds before putting her hands on his shoulders to get his attention. Like her, he had confetti and tidbits of string in his hair, but to her, he was the sexiest man she'd ever seen, and her thundering pulse refused to be ignored.

Standing on tiptoe to speak into Gere's ear, Shelley said, "There's a more common New Year's custom that comes to mind."

Wondering what she meant, Gere looked around, slightly overwhelmed at the seemingly endless activity in every direction: the conga line, people shooting party string, people with arms linked, singing, some couples clinking plastic drink cups together in a toast to the new day. And then he noticed the kissing couples—one couple here, another there, clinging tightly to each other and kissing as though there were no tomorrow.

Kissing. Of course. Gere did everything but slap his forehead at his own obtuseness. But then, it would have been impossible to slap his forehead when both his hands suddenly were so industriously occupied caressing Shelley's waist, pulling her close, while his entire conscious mind was focused on the luscious mouth tilted invitingly toward his. It wasn't that kissing Shelley hadn't crossed Gere's mind, it was simply that thinking of kissing Shelley had become his normal state of mind every time he was within fifty feet of her. Thinking of kissing her seemed to be a new way of life for him.

He lowered his mouth to hers with deliberate slowness, first sampling its lushness, then plundering its depths. Never had a kiss been more involving, more inflammatory. They were nudged and shoved by the teeming crowd, but Gere took no notice. The manic furor of the celebration going on around them was now irrelevant. Shelley was the only thing that mattered to him: holding her, feeling her next to him, tasting her. He was driven to claim her, possess her, absorb her into him, lose himself in her.

Gere and Shelley were so involved in each other, so oblivious to the hoopla surrounding them, that Stanley's wild whoop of joy scarcely registered with them. But Wild Stanley refused to be ignored, and clasping Gere's shoulder, wrested him from Shelley, tearing him away from the kiss.

Gere blinked at him uncomprehendingly. "Congratulate me!" Stanley shouted. "I'm going to be a papa!"

"A papa?" Gere echoed, still fuzzy-headed as he accepted Stanley's right hand to shake it.

Shelley was the first to catch his meaning, and turned to give Barbara a hug. "A baby? Oh, Barbara, how wonderful!"

Maggie turned it into a three-way hug. "And you didn't say a thing! Not a thing!"

"I wanted Stanley to be the first to know," Barbara explained. "And I wanted to wait until his birthday."

"Hey, give her back," Stanley said, grabbing one of Barbara's hands and playfully pulling her away from the women. He patted her abdomen for emphasis, grinned broadly and added, "Hot damn! A kid!"

"And I didn't know how he'd take the news," Barbara exclaimed, glowing in the light of Stanley's joy.

"This calls for a celebration," Stanley said. "I'm buying."

They wove through the crowd to the Adventurer's Club, which was a cool, serene contrast to the other clubs they'd been in. Passing tuxedoed butlers and an occasional British explorer in khaki safari clothes and a monocle, they found a relatively secluded corner and ordered soft drinks.

"I should have known something was up when Barbara didn't drink wine tonight," Stanley said, and pinned his wife with a sardonic look. "Dieting, huh? Since when have you ever gone on a diet?"

After the appropriate toasts and more hugs and gushing well wishes, Stanley suggested they go back to the dance club to continue the celebration. "I feel like dancing all night." He sobered suddenly and turned to Barbara. "If you feel up to it. I mean, it's okay, isn't it?"

Barbara grinned. "Yes, I can dance. And I feel like celebrating, too. After all, it's your thirtieth birthday."

"So?" Stanley said delightedly. "Do we party?"

Maggie raised her eyebrow inquiringly at Roger, who shrugged. "Sure!" she agreed. "Let's party."

All eyes turned to Shelley and Gere. Shelley debated what to do. She was happy for Barbara, but Barbara and Stanley were going to celebrate whether alone or in a crowd. And Stanley's brash announcement had interrupted something she'd like to resume. She looked at Gere, and then back at Stanley and Barbara. "I, uh... Look, guys, it's late, and I've got a bit of a headache. If you don't mind..."

So, with final hugs and good wishes for Barbara and Stanley, she took Gere's hand and they left the park together.

Gere was quiet as they walked, preoccupied with the events of the evening and trying to interpret them, especially Shelley's reaction to Barbara's news and her headache. When she'd as much as asked him to kiss her and then kissed him as though he were a long-lost lover, he'd hoped— But then, just when he'd been hoping the evening would end with their own private form of fireworks, she'd announced that she had a headache.

Disappointment settled into a hollow ache in his chest. What if he'd misinterpreted everything? What if he wasn't special to her at all? What if he was just her Saturday-night date? But even as self-preservation forced him to consider all the possibilities, to be prepared for any eventuality, he discounted them.

The party girl with the annual pass to Pleasure Island had a headache at half-past midnight on the Saturday night she went out with Garrick Booth. Yet the way she kissed him was special. He couldn't be imagining the intangibles that distinguished those kisses from ordinary kisses. They were too...extraordinary. And he couldn't prove scientifically that the intangibles existed, but he knew they existed with the same instinctual certainty with which a caterpillar knows he must make himself a cocoon.

Strange, how much better he understood instinct since meeting Shelley. He'd understood it on an intellectual level before, observed its manifestations in the insects he studied; he'd read about it, even written about it. But until he'd met Shelley, he'd never fully appreciated the sheer strength of instinctive yearning. He'd wanted before—wanted toys as a child, good grades as a student, recognition as a professional. He'd even wanted women. But all those wants grew out of the logical need for acceptance or recognition. Even his desire for women was logical, since it was so obviously influenced by a biological need.

His reaction to Shelley was rooted in that vast gray area that existed beyond logic, beyond precise definition, beyond scientific scrutiny. He simply—or, more precisely, complexly—reacted to her. He desired her. He yearned for her. Because of her, he was thinking of things he'd never given any consideration to before: mating for life, sharing lives, creating lives.

Yes, even that. He, Garrick Booth, who'd congratulated his buddies when they became fathers with much the same detached sentiment that he'd observed insects coupling to create yet another cycle of life, had watched a near stranger pat his wife's belly and found himself wondering what it would be like to have a woman tell him she carried his child inside her.

He, Garrick Booth, who'd long viewed procreation as the means to perpetuation of a species, had wondered what it must be like to anticipate the birth of a child—not simply a new generation of a species and yet another combination of inherited genetic traits, but a human being with a name and a face and a personality.

It was a lot to think about.

Gere was uncommonly silent in the car. Shelley wondered what had him so preoccupied. He'd been attentive all evening. Why, with the prospect of being alone imminent, did he now have to seem so remote? Except to ask whether she preferred the top up or down, he hadn't spoken at all since they left the park.

She almost wished she'd told him not to bother putting the top down. Somehow having the sky above them, with nothing separating them from the stars except light-years of distance, made Gere's silence more ominous, almost like a rebellion against the intimate rapport they'd established under the stars the week before. But Gere's silence aside, it was a beautiful night, so she tilted her head back, closed her eyes and enjoyed the wind on her face.

Finally they reached her duplex, and Gere pulled into her driveway and cut the car's engine. The resulting silence loomed overlong before Gere said, "How's your head?"

"My head?"

"Your headache."

"Oh, that," she said. Poor baby, he'd believed her! It hadn't dawned on him that she'd been making an excuse so she could be alone with him. Either she'd been misreading his signals, or he was totally obtuse to hers.

Could he possibly be that naive? She looked at Gere, with his consciously faddish hairstyle and his sympathetic eyes, and exhaled a sigh. If there'd been a farm in her family to bet, she'd have bet the family farm that he could be just that naive.

His hands were still on the steering wheel. Feeling her heart turning to mush again, she put her hand over his and said, "Why don't you come in for a while?"

8

"ARE YOU SURE? Your head—"

"I think we need to talk."

Not knowing whether "needing to talk" was a good sign or a bad one, Gere nodded.

"Would you like something to drink?" she asked. "Coffee, herb tea, white wine..."

Gere chose coffee because it would take the longest to make and, thus, bought him time. If he was about to get what was commonly referred to as a brush-off, at least it wouldn't be a quick one. Following her into the kitchen he watched her spoon coffee grounds into a filter, and measure water into the coffeemaker.

He was never quite prepared for the effects her beauty had on him. It mesmerized him. There she was, all female, with that miniskirt hugging her behind and her legs shown to full advantage. They weren't the long sleek legs of a model, but they were gorgeous and gracefully curved, like the rest of her body. He couldn't look at her without noticing those uncompromisingly female curves—her bust, the nip of her waist, the swell of her hips and that lovely behind now so caressingly encased in denim.

Shelley took meticulous care in making the coffee, stalling for time. She wasn't sure how to broach the subject she'd invited him to discuss. Some women might have the chutzpah just to look at him and say, "I lied about the headache because I wanted to be alone with you so we could make love, so how about it, big boy?"

Some women might have that chutzpah. Shelley Peters did not. Shelley Peters had a chest filled with mush where her heart should be, a stomach filled with butterflies, a lump the size of a small third-world country stuck in her throat, an aching longing a few inches below her waist and a case of nerves she hoped didn't turn into hives.

All things considered, she figured she must be in love. Admitting that, however, didn't tell her how to get the conversation going in the right direction.

Gere was beginning to suspect that Shelley didn't have a headache, had never had one. To him, that meant she was probably going to serve up some bad news—gently, tactfully, of course—with the coffee. He was not reassured when she took a package of cookies from the pantry and meticulously arranged them on a plate. Suspense knotted his gut as he dreaded the gentle boot out the door. *"It was all very nice, but . . . don't call me, I'll call you." Then there'd be waves from the mailbox occasionally, like those of a picnicker tossing crusts to birds.*

Gere was a patient man when it came to detailed scientific observation. He was not a patient man when he believed he was about to be brushed off over coffee and cookies. He decided to call her bluff. "Shouldn't you take something for your head? Aspirin, or something?"

Her back was to him, and he saw her shoulders stiffen momentarily, sag as she exhaled a sigh, then stiffen again in resolve as she turned and met his gaze evenly. "I don't have a headache, Gere. I never did."

He'd thought he was prepared, but all he could manage to say was, "Oh."

Shelley approached the table, sat down in the chair closest to his and grasped his hand between hers. Gere felt as though his midsection were about to be split open with an ax, and steeled himself against the blow, thinking it would be more humane of her not to touch him while she was tactfully sweeping him out the door.

"This isn't easy for me," she said.

Did she think it was easy for him to sit there and listen to what she was about to say?

Shelley sensed his tension. If only he'd cooperate a little, give her some sign of encouragement. *If only he'd pull her into his lap and kiss her as though there were no tomorrow...*

She tried again, leaping in because there seemed no way to be subtle. "Gere, usually by the time I've been out with a man twice, it's pretty obvious where we're headed. I mean—" She released a frustrated sigh, and then a spate of nervous laughter. "Actually, it's probably pretty fair to say that by the time a man kisses me the way you kissed me tonight, he's the one who suggests coming inside, if you get my drift."

She frowned. "You're not getting my drift at all, are you?" But she didn't give him time to reply before chattering on nervously. "The truth is, I don't have a headache at all. I only said I did because I wanted . . . I mean, I thought you wanted to be alone with me, and if you did, then I wanted to be alone with you, too. But now I'm not so sure whether it's what you want, and I really wish you'd say something before I make a bigger fool of myself than I have already."

A deafening silence followed. Finally, after what seemed an eternity, Gere sprang out of his chair so abruptly that it almost overturned. Giving her hand a tug, he coaxed her to stand also, then cradled her face in his hands. "You want to know if I'd like to make love to you?"

This time, it was Gere who gave Shelley no chance to reply. The expression in his eyes was so compelling, so intense, that Shelley couldn't have looked away if fire alarms had suddenly sounded in the next room, and his voice was taut with hard-fought control as he said, "I don't think it's possible for a man to want a woman more than I want you at this moment."

As much as she would have loved to be cool and sophisticated and able to say something witty, she felt none of those things. Cool? She was burning, set on fire by the raw desire in his eyes. Witty? She had no wit left; he'd drained wit and logic right out of her, leaving only mindless longing. Sophisticated? All she could do was gulp, trying to dislodge the lump that seemed to have taken up permanent residence in her throat.

Seconds passed, grew into minutes. Finally Gere said, self-consciously, "So, what do we do now?"

Shelley had regained enough of her wits to reply, "I think I should turn off the coffeepot." Then, realizing that might sound a bit off-center, she added, "I'm not much in the mood for coffee anymore, are you?"

Gere appeared as awestruck and overwhelmed as Shelley felt as he shook his head.

Shelley stalked to the coffeemaker, turned it off and looked at Gere. There they were, on opposite sides of the small kitchen, she with her back to the counter, he with his back to the table.

We're skittish as ponies, Shelley thought, wondering how to escape the horrid impasse at which they'd arrived. She was about to say his name, when he said hers instead.

"Shelley." The way he said it made it sound important, revered. She widened her eyes to indicate she was listening.

"There's nothing wrong with me," he said somberly, then, after a pause, muttered a curse. "This is more embarrassing than I ever—" He drew in a fortifying breath and swore again in pure disgust. "What I mean is, I'm perfectly normal, and, I'm certainly ready—" He groaned. "Holy cow, Shelley, if I was any readier to make love to you, I'd probably spontaneously combust. It's just that—"

With an exhausted sigh, he dropped into the nearest chair. Shelley crossed the room in two strides and sat next to him, scooping her hands into his. "Gere."

"I cut my hair and learned how to dance, Shelley, but for the life of me, I don't know what to do next. I've only made love to one woman in my entire life, and that was different. It was mostly— She sort of took control, and I was just along for the ride. I didn't care about her. I mean, I cared, but not . . ."

He sighed again, and squeezed her hands. "Damn it, Shelley, I don't want to screw this up. Help me along, would you?"

"Like I'm light-years ahead of you in experience," Shelley muttered, slightly overwhelmed by the irony of the situation. True, she could top one, but her record wasn't *all that* more impressive.

Gere looked at her. "Hmm?"

She shook her head. "Nothing. Just—" Smiling slyly, she guided his hand to her mouth and pressed several tiny kisses on the back of it. "You've been doing just fine up to now. I don't think you need any help from me."

"But I don't know how to get from here to . . . where we want to wind up."

Shelley shook her head and sighed. The heart-to-mush maker was at it again. "I know you're brilliant, Gere, but sometimes you think too much."

"But . . ."

"Making love isn't something you choreograph, it's something you feel."

Gere raised his free hand to her neck, curving his fingers around that alluring column and caressing the tender area just under her ear with his thumb. "Believe me, sweetheart, I'm feeling it."

"Then why don't we dance?" she said, rising.

"Dance?"

"It worked at the nightclub—at least, it worked for me."

It worked again. Gere's arms and "St. James Infirmary" proved to be a sexually lethal combination. All Shelley had to do was close her eyes and cuddle her cheek against Gere's shoulder and she was back under the stars, at the club, at the stage with fireworks going off overhead. Only this time, they were alone. There would be no cops to shine lights in their faces, no attendants to clear their throats and make wisecracks, no friends with announcements of impending births. Sliding her arms around his waist, she rested her hands on his hips.

"Did you really learn to dance just for tonight?" she asked.

"I hadn't planned to tell you about that."

"Why not?" she cooed back, her whisper a gale-force puff of stimulation as it wafted into his ear.

He shrugged gently. "I guess I was embarrassed at not knowing how already."

"How did you learn?"

"Videos from the library."

Shelley chuckled against his shoulder.

"That's why I wasn't going to tell you," he said.

Shelley ran her palms up his spine, then splayed her hands over his shoulder muscles and kneaded them, taking pleasure from the feel of powerful sinew under her fingertips. "That's the most romantic thing a man's ever done for me."

"And worth every second I put into it," Gere murmured, burying his face in her hair. He wouldn't have believed it possible to be aware of a woman in so many ways and so many places at the same time. He felt like one sensitized nerve ending from head to toe, with her hair under his cheek, her breasts compressed against his chest, her hands doing remarkable things to his back and her thighs chafing his as they moved together to the music. The rest he dared not think about, for fear of losing sanity and control in one fell swoop.

"Videos from the library," she said, nibbling at his neck. "Who'd have believed it?"

"Mrs. Northbrook said that wanting to hold you would make it easier. She was right."

Shelley almost asked who Mrs. Northbrook was, but every female instinct in her told her she had nothing to fear in the answer, so she decided not to risk disrupting the mood. Instead, she kissed a trail from his neck, along his jaw, to his lips. "Kiss me," she entreated. "Make love to me."

Gere knew in that instant that everything was going to be all right. How could he have been nervous about being with Shelley? Excited, stimulated, lustful, maybe; tender, perhaps; but nervous? Never! Not with the kindest human being on the face of the earth.

Kiss me. Make love to me. He obliged her with his mouth, covering hers, gently at first, then fiercely, hungrily, insatiably. He obliged her with his hands, exploring, caressing, massaging her body. Most of all, he obliged her with his heart, gifting her with tenderness, with sensitivity, with love. *Love.* The lovemaking she'd asked for, the love he freely offered.

She made it easy for him, at times suggesting, at times simply showing him by leading the way. Before he could worry about how they would get there, she had subtly steered him to the bedroom. Before he could worry about the next step, she was unbuttoning his shirt. And then her fingers were combing through the hair on his chest, and Gere felt as if he'd stumbled off the edge of reality and landed in a corner of heaven.

He reached for the buttons at the front of her shirt— the row of tiny buttons that had teased and tortured him all evening—and found the top button perversely obstinate. Shelley stayed his hand with hers and laughed softly. "It doesn't come open."

His perplexity must have been obvious, because she laughed again. "They're ornamental. It's a pullover. See?"

Gere saw. Oh, and what a view, when she pulled the shirt over her head and then released the front clasp of her bra. Upon seeing, he had to touch, and upon touching, he had to kiss. After kissing, he touched again, feasting on the sight of his hands on those luxuriant mounds of flesh, and then on the sight of Shelley's face, and the dreamy expression in her eyes.

The effect of his touch on her flesh, Gere thought, awed by the knowledge that he could arouse in her the same sort of splendor she produced in him. He embraced her fully, and groaned in ecstasy at the sensation of their bare chests melded together. Eyes closed, he burrowed his face in her hair, absorbing the intensity of the pleasure of holding her. Her back was smooth as satin, soft as velvet under his fingers, while her hands spread the fire of passion with each caress of his shoulders, his spine.

"I think it's time I excused myself," she said, her voice as vaporous as a cloud.

Excuse herself? Leave? It was incomprehensible, unthinkable.

She drew away, far enough to see his face. "There's—uh—no graceful way to remove panty hose," she said. "A minute in the bathroom will buy me a lot of dignity."

Before leaving the bedroom, she went to the bed and folded back the covers. The gesture was erotic, a potent blend of suggestion and invitation. He couldn't take his eyes off Shelley as long as she was in the room, equally mesmerized by the sight of her breasts as she approached him, and the graceful lines of her back as she passed from view. Then he found himself staring at her bed, with its lush comforter, pastel yellow blanket and floral sheet doubled back, the plumped pillows and smooth, flower-splashed mattress waiting to embrace him and Shelley as they became lovers.

He sat on the edge of the bed and inhaled deeply. He might have expected his ardor to cool somewhat when she was away, but his body tensed, harder than ever from the sheer anticipation of crawling between the cool sheets with her.

After a moment spent sitting in statuelike immobility, he bent and unlaced his shoes. High-tops were a damned sight more complicated to remove than panty hose, he'd wager, although, of course, he'd never had any personal experience with the latter. He pressed his socked feet into the carpet and wiggled his toes, relieved to be out of the clodhoppers.

Shelley had been gone too long. He missed her. Just as her presence soothed and reassured him, her absence made him uneasy and uncertain. Left with time to think, he found himself pondering the foil pouch in his billfold, and his promise to Kelsey to be responsible.

Just when his thoughts were turning gloomy with doubt, Shelley waltzed back into the room, smiling shyly, shattering his doubts like so many soap bubbles. She tossed a similar foil pouch onto the bed, near the pillows, and said, "A little something for you to put on later."

Gere stood and opened his arms. She raced into them, hugging him tightly, clinging to him. It was the first inkling he'd had that she was as nervous, in her own way, as he was, and the realization of his own insensitivity shocked him. He said her name—soothingly, as an apology—and she lifted her face for his kiss.

His awareness of the world telescoped into an awareness of the woman nestled in his arms, of the sensations she evoked when she touched him, of the way she responded to his touch, of the ways she opened to him.

He felt her hands between them—her fingers inside the waistband of his trousers, then pulling down the zipper. He inhaled sharply as she splayed her open hands over his buttocks, then gasped as she shoved his pants down, over his hips, and brushed them farther, past his knees. He kicked out of them when they bunched at his ankles, trying to remember to breathe as she slid her fingertips up and down his bare thighs in long, teasing, strokes—*almost* moving into the sensitive area just above and between; *almost* caressing that hot, pulsating part of him still throbbing with longing for her touch.

He wanted to scream in frustration when she withdrew her hands entirely—until she looped her arms around his neck and, while giving him a deep, probing kiss, leaped up, wrapping her legs around his waist.

The miniskirt crawled up her thighs, leaving only her panties and his briefs separating them. Gere reeled with the sudden shock of the intimate contact, then recovered, clinging to her, supporting her with his hands on her behind. Cursing the denim bunched under his palms, he took a step back and sat down on the bed with Shelley in his lap. Every tiny move she made was a taunt and a torment, inflaming him, frustrating him, driving him mad.

Groaning in frustration, Shelley extricated her fingers from his hair and arched her midsection away, reaching between them to adjust the zipper on her skirt. "I thought since you didn't get to do the buttons, you might want to do the honors with the skirt, so I left it on."

Gere's hands were trembling as much as hers as he tried to help with the zipper. Finally, their joint efforts paid off. Leaning away from him, Shelley guided the skirt down her legs and, with a voluptuous laugh, tossed it aside.

Oddly, with that major barrier so cavalierly disposed of, their lovemaking turned gentle again. Cuddled together under the covers, they caressed almost lazily, exploring and discovering, until the tension between them built again to a fevered pitch and, at last, they dispatched the final barriers between them.

Naked, lying side by side on the bed, they locked gazes and suffered a moment of shocked silence pregnant with the knowledge of what they were about to do and the question of how best to proceed. Then, with restless impatience, Shelley reached out to curl her fingers around Gere's erection.

Gere groaned, his frustration an actual, physical ache as she stroked and kneaded him with fingers of magic and fire.

"Me, too," she whispered, as he chafed the tips of her breasts with his palms. "Oh, Gere."

Her hand ceased its ministrations, and she grew so still that Gere could hear her breathing. "Shelley?"

Turning her head, she placed a kiss on the tender area where his neck met his shoulder. "It's time you tried out that new wardrobe."

It isn't awkward at all, Gere thought incredulously as she rolled the condom over his erection. Like everything else with Shelley, safe sex seemed like the most natural thing in the world.

They embraced, stroked, kissed, caressed; and they coupled in a joining that was gentle and tumultuous, fiery and splendid. When at last they fell away from each other, sated and exhausted, still breathing heavily, Gere expelled her name on a ragged exhalation.

"Hmm?" Shelley responded cautiously.

"Wow!" Gere said.

Shelley laughed weakly. "Thank goodness!"

"For what?" Gere asked.

"When you said my name that way, I was certain you were going to say thank-you."

"I thought I was."

"No. You said, 'Wow!' with an exclamation point."

"Is that better?"

Shelley closed her eyes and sighed, her breath hot against his shoulder. "It's . . . *eons and eons* better."

Gere found the energy to push up on one elbow so he could see her face. "Why?"

"Think about it, Gere. 'Thank you,' sounds very polite and very proper. 'Wow!' says so much more. You're a Harvard man. You have a Ph.D."

"Two Ph.D.'s, actually."

"Two? Oh, right. Well, that's even better. Just think about it—I reduced a man with two Ph.D.'s from Harvard to 'Wow!' That's like Walter Cronkite."

Gere rolled his eyes exasperatedly. "You've lost me, Shelley. I'm still back at 'Wow!' What has Walter Cronkite got to do with anything?"

"I saw this documentary on TV, about famous live reactions, like when the Hindenberg blew up, and the announcer got so hysterical and almost started crying, and when that streaker went running across the stage during the Academy Awards and David Niven made some witty remark.

"Anyway, Walter Cronkite had been covering the space program since the very first satellite, but when the first astronaut stepped out onto the moon, he was so awed that all he could say was, 'Oh, gee!' I mean, he was the most trusted man in America—they took a poll—and he had all those years of experience on camera, and all he could say was, 'Oh, gee!' So, you see, making love with me was almost as good for you as men walking on the moon was for Walter Cronkite."

Gere was sorely tempted to tell her that hers was the screwiest logic he'd ever heard in the whole of his thirty years. Instead, he grinned like the lovestruck lunatic she'd turned him into and said, "Sex with you was better for me than actually walking on the moon would have been for Walter Cronkite."

Shelley's eyes widened and got suspiciously bright. Clamping her hands on either side of his face, she murmured, "Oh, gee!" before pulling his mouth into kissing range.

9

"WHAT'S YOUR OTHER Ph.D. in? Besides entomology,"
Shelley asked. After making love a second time, they
had dozed, then awakened and made love yet again.
Now they were cuddled in her bed, totally oblivious to
the hour, having neither energy nor inclination to check
the clock.

"Actually, entomology is my second Ph.D.," Gere
answered. "I started out in chemistry, like my grandfather."

"Your grandfather was a chemist?"

Gere nodded. "During the golden age of chemistry.
He helped develop some of the earliest processes for
making plastics."

"Is that what you wanted to do? Make plastics?"

"Just the opposite. By the time I got to college, we
were beginning to get a glimpse of what plastics were
doing to the environment. I decided it was time someone worked on damage control."

"Out to save the world?"

Gere grinned. "Aren't most eighteen-year-olds?"

"I suppose the ones that aren't out to party it to death
are," Shelley said, yawning gently and nuzzling her
cheek against his chest. "So how did you get from
chemistry to bugs?"

"I became enchanted with the subject of naturally-
occurring chemicals, and I found out about some research being done using insect secretions and volun-

teered to do some of the grunt work and then got hooked. I started taking entomology courses and the hours started mounting, and before I knew it, I had my master's and was working on a second Ph.D."

"I envy you."

Gere experienced a stab of guilt. He'd always been a little embarrassed and defensive about his family's affluence. Plastics seemed a ridiculous way for a person to have made a fortune, but his grandfather had been wise enough to get everything he worked on properly protected by patent, and had prospered accordingly. "Because I went to Harvard?" he asked.

"Not particularly," Shelley replied. "More for finding something that fascinated you and following through on it. I've found so many things fascinating, I've never been able to focus on one of them long enough to really accomplish anything with it. My parents would give their eye teeth for me to have a degree in something, instead of a collection of report cards and certificates of completion."

"Degrees aren't all that important."

Shelley laughed. "From a man with two Ph.D.'s. From Haa-vaad."

Gere laughed at her playful mockery of the pronunciation. "What I meant was, you have a job that you like and find fulfilling. What difference would a piece of paper make?"

He heard himself saying it, but couldn't believe it was his voice. If his colleagues could hear him, they'd probably think he'd unraveled one cocoon too many. Any research scientist knew the value of degrees. Degrees meant funding and grants. Degrees were credibility. A scientist was the sum of his degrees, his school, his publication history and his work.

"It would make a difference to my mom," Shelley explained. "I was the first one to actually enroll in college. Ken didn't want to do anything but work on engines, so he went to trade school, and Libby didn't want to do anything but get married and raise babies, so she got by on the business classes she'd taken in high school. So when I enrolled in college, Mom was really excited. Only I couldn't settle on a major, and the counselors got upset, and I didn't do too well in math or French One—"

"French One?"

"The foreign language requirement. Anyway, it seemed like I was wasting a lot of time learning stuff I didn't care about, and when I found a class I really liked, it wasn't leading to anything, so I dropped out and became a specialty-class junkie. Now the heat's on Kevin."

"The lizard master."

"Mmm-hmm. And you know what? I think he'll do it. He loves school, and he's curious about everything. Right now, he wants to become an entomologist."

"He does?"

"Mmm-hmm. He has ever since you sent him the beetles for Annabel, and I told him what you do. He thinks it would be neat to have a job where you could have frogs and catch bugs."

Gere kissed the top of her head. "You'll have to bring him out to the institute one day, let him look over the equipment and some of the experiments in progress."

"He would love that," Shelley said, snuggling again. "So would I."

She grew silent, and Gere thought perhaps she'd fallen asleep, until she exhaled the gentlest of sighs and said, "Tonight has been like a dream."

He knew from the change in her breathing exactly when she did drift off, and he stroked her hair, wishing he could hit some kind of cosmic button and freeze the richness of that particular moment. The scientist in him checked the clock, making a mental note of the time: five-seventeen in the morning. He lay there until six, wide-awake, then eased his arm out from under her neck and made his achy way to the bathroom, gathering clothes along the way.

As quietly as possible, he freshened up and dressed. Without the gel and special brush the stylist had showed him how to use, all Gere could do was comb his hair smooth with his pocket comb and hope it dried well. A few weeks ago, he wouldn't have paused in front of the mirror more than a second or two, but today he studied his reflection critically, from his wet hair to his hopelessly wrinkled shirt and pants. *Some dream lover!*

The bathroom wasn't particularly small, but it was filled with Shelley's things—personal articles, the soap she used, female things that made her look and smell good. The walls seemed to be closing in on him as he stared at his reflection. *Would the real Gere Booth please step forward? Last night, Shelley had made love to a hunk; now he hoped he could slip away without her waking up enough to discover that the hunk was really a frog.*

Kneeling beside the bed, he woke her with tiny kisses on her forehead. Her unconsciously sensual groan teased his raw nerve endings. "You're not in bed anymore," she said groggily. "What time is it, anyway?"

"A little after six—"

"Six?"

"I have to get home, Shelley. The dogs—"

She pushed herself up on one elbow. "Oh."

"They're on the patio. Von Frisch would be all right, but Wigglesworth's liable to shove his way through the screening if he's left alone too long."

She collapsed back onto the pillow wearily. "How did you say those dogs got those ridiculous names?"

"Famous entomologists," Gere told her. "When I went to pick out a puppy, I chose Wigglesworth first. He was so hyper, the name just seemed to suit him."

"And von Frisch?"

"The breeder knew I wanted a pair, and he kept saying, 'Now you need to choose a bitch.' It's an official breeder's term, you know."

She nodded, and yawned. "Mmm-hmm."

"Since I'd named the male after an entomologist, I wanted to name the female after one, too, and the breeder was there, pointing out pups saying, 'That's a bitch,' and 'That one's a bitch,' and it just struck me as funny, and I thought about von Frisch and it almost rhymed. *Von Frisch, the bitch.* No one else has ever caught on, but it was funny at the time, and the name stuck."

"Who was von Frisch, anyway?"

"Karl von Frisch? He was the first researcher to discover the honeybee dance language."

"Of course," Shelley mumbled into the pillow. "Should have known."

Gere kissed her again. "Can I see you later? Dinner, maybe?"

"Sure," she replied. "But it'll have to be someplace simple, so we can break it off early. I've got to sort mail first thing in the morning."

"I'll call you later," Gere said, dropping a final kiss on the tip of her nose.

He was all the way to the bedroom door when she said, "Gere?" He arched an eyebrow. "Don't you want my phone number?"

He quoted it, one digit at a time, and then shrugged away her frown. "I looked it up once."

"No one should be so brilliant before seven in the morning," she complained, burrowing down into her pillow.

Gere laughed aloud as he made his way to the front door.

GERE WAS WAITING FOR her at the mailbox, just as he had on Monday and Tuesday.

Shelley grinned. *Right on the mark, Dr. Garrick Genius-Hunk Booth. Now pick up on your cue. It's time to pull me into your arms, kiss me like a crazed sex maniac, and tell me you can't possibly wait until the weekend to make love to me again.*

It had to be his idea, of course. She couldn't possibly tell him how much she was aching to feel his arms around her. Her ego was still smarting from how quickly he'd agreed with her suggestion that it would be best to confine their time alone to the weekends because of her work schedule. No, she wasn't going to give him the satisfaction of being the one to suggest they throw logic to the winds and succumb to passion's urgency. No way.

Of course, after he'd convinced her he couldn't last another three days without spending some time with her, and *begged* her to see him, even though she had to be at work early the next day, she'd be more than willing to give him another type of satisfaction—

He kissed her as soon as the Jeep had stopped, and she kissed him back enthusiastically enough to give him the confidence that she would be receptive to his grov-eling. She could literally feel his reluctance to pull away from the kiss in the tension of his muscles.

"Good afternoon, Dr. Booth," she said, with mock primness. "How's the insect-watching business?"

His frown, so unexpected, hit her like a physical blow. "It's going very well," he said, the words in op-position to the pained expression on his face. "In fact—"

Shelley steeled herself for bad news.

"I need to explain—" he continued, the words ob-viously inflicting pain as they crawled haltingly from his throat.

"Yes?" Shelley prompted, trying to sound under-standing when, in reality, she felt as though someone had jerked the rug out from under her. This was *not* going as she'd imagined it. Not at all.

"The moths are mating," he said.

So? Shelley thought in frustration. That wasn't ex-actly a news flash. Anyone who'd ever hung cedar chips in their closet or packed away winter clothes in moth balls knew that the little buggers mated and multiplied far too quickly for the public good.

"Shelley, I have a whole batch of males that I raised on controlled diets in the caterpillar stage. You remem-ber—we talked about the influence of diet on chemical attractants, and the premise that female moths select mates according to their ability to ensure survival for the offspring."

"Oh. That. Sure, I remember." At the time, all that talk about mate selection had seemed like foreplay; now it was beginning to sound more like a kiss off.

"The point is, the mating season is limited, and it's imperative that I get the males I've raised to female moths when they're . . . *receptive.*"

Shelley felt her heart dissolve to mush again as he blushed endearingly, even as his message began to sink in. "And exactly *when* are the little girl moths receptive?" she asked, aiming for wit and hitting sarcasm instead.

"In the evenings. Beginning at dusk. What I'm trying to say is, they don't take weekends off, so I can't, either. At least not *this* weekend."

"Oh," Shelley said, hiding her disappointment. If she was going to be involved with a scientist, she *had* to be the soul of understanding about his work.

Intellectually she understood that timing was critical in his research, and that if this particular moth mated at a specific time of year, at a specific time of day, Gere had to be there. But it seemed only fair that if Gere was there for the horny little moths Monday through Friday, he could "be there" for *her* on Saturday night, since that would be their only night to do what he would be observing the moths doing the rest of the week.

With her heart ripping into tiny pieces, she swallowed her pride and the lump of rejection in her throat. "Maybe we could see each other during the day, instead," she said, finding the role of understanding lover a long stretch. "Kevin's school carnival is Saturday. You could come with us."

"I don't think—"

"Kevin's anxious to meet you," she coaxed. "I agreed to work a shift at one of the booths, but that would only be for a while. It would be fun."

"It's not— I've got some things I have to tend to Saturday afternoon," he said. "But . . . what time does the carnival start? Maybe you could bring Kevin by here for a tour of the institute Saturday morning."

A Saturday-morning tour of the institute with her baby brother in tow didn't sound to Shelley like a very fair trade for an afternoon of silliness at a carnival, but she forced her lips into a smile over her gritted teeth, until she'd found enough control to say, "I'm sure Kevin would love that. If you're sure it won't be an imposition."

"It's not. I just . . . I'm not used to kids. I wouldn't want to turn a promising scientist off the idea of science."

"There's not a chance of that," Shelley assured him. "All you have to do is show him your frogs and a few crawly things, and you'll have a convert for life." *You've already made a convert of his big sister.*

A very long, awkward silence followed, during which Gere developed an inordinate interest in the toe of his tattered sneakers. He didn't look up to ask, "You're not . . . upset, are you? That I have to work this weekend?"

"Don't be ridiculous!" Shelley replied, still trying to sound like the soul of understanding. "It's not as though you could ask the moths to punch a time clock."

"No," he agreed quickly. "Of course. I can't do that."

"Well," Shelley said, when another strained silence threatened to become unbearably long.

"I know," Gere said resolutely, leaning forward to give her a quick parting kiss on the lips. "You have mail to deliver."

Shelley deliberately gunned the Jeep's engine. "Just like you have moths to watch."

Maybe if she had wings and sweated chemical sexual attractants, he would find time to watch her on the weekends.

"YOU HAVE TO SHOW ONE little boy around the institute, and that's big trouble?" Kelsey asked.

"But I don't know anything about kids," Gere countered, marveling at his sister's inability to grasp the scope of the situation.

He heard Kelsey's sniff of exasperation on the other end of the line. "I hate to be a radical, Gere, but did it occur to you that kids are just human beings who haven't grown up yet?"

"But it's Shelley's brother," Gere said.

"I wasn't aware she came from a mutant strain of some kind."

"Very funny, Kelsey."

"Look, Gere. The kid has a pet lizard and thinks studying bugs is neat. Sounds like a typical boy, to me."

"But, what do I say to him?"

"Just *talk* to him. Point out anything interesting and answer his questions. Just avoid the heavy-duty scientific words, the way you would with any nonscientist. You'll live through it, trust me. I'm surrounded by little darlings every day, and I've survived just fine."

"How are your health/sex-education classes shaping up?"

Kelsey exhaled wearily. "I'm still working on them. In fact, that's what I was doing when the phone rang."

"Lesson plans on a Friday night?" He was genuinely surprised.

"Oho! My big brother finds himself a girlfriend, and suddenly I'm a wallflower if I'm not out partying every weekend."

"I didn't mean—"

"It's okay. I could think of more exciting ways to be passing my time, but I didn't have any plans, and the research materials were sitting here, waiting. Enough about work. Back to Shelley. If she's bringing her brother over, your date must have gone all right."

"Better than that. It was—" Words failed him.

"Say no more. Please. I can hear the vibrating of Cupid's bow in the background as you speak."

"She's not after my money," he said defiantly.

Kelsey paused before replying. "So, what *is* wrong?"

"She thinks I'm a hunk."

"So you made it to hunkdom. What's the problem?"

There were times when Gere wished Kelsey weren't quite so perceptive. He wasn't sure whether this was one of them, or whether he'd used Shelley's brother's impending visit as an excuse to call Kelsey, hoping she would make him talk about what was really on his mind.

"I'm not really a hunk, Kelsey! Don't you think Shelley's going to notice sooner or later?"

The other end of the line turned deadly silent and remained that way a long time. Finally Kelsey responded, "Gere, if this girl doesn't like you for the person you are instead of the clothes you wear, then the sooner you cut loose from her, the better off you're going to be."

"But I don't want to cut her loose," Gere said. "I want her—"

To love me, he finished silently. And then, because he had to lash out at someone, he challenged Kelsey: "If that's the way you felt about it, why did you set me up? Why did you pester me to death about cutting my hair and buying the right clothes? Why did you make such a big deal over my goddamned glasses?"

"So that you would have the confidence to go after what you wanted!" Kelsey snapped back. "And, damn it, it worked! Except that now you're afraid she's fallen in love with Frankenstein's monster instead of Frankenstein himself!"

"Frankenstein's monster, huh? Well, at least I had the right shoes for it."

"You bought high-tops!" Kelsey said delightedly.

"Yes, I did. And I didn't step on her toe once in those clodhoppers, either!"

After another thoughtful pause, Kelsey said, softly, "If this girl doesn't love you, she's nuts."

"She's a little nuts, anyway," Gere replied, and before Kelsey had a chance to jump on that disclosure with both feet, asked, "You're a coach—have you ever had your players imagine they were going to win?"

"You mean visualization?"

"That's it."

"Sure. It works wonders when a team needs a little boost of confidence."

"You're as nuts as she is."

"It must be a female thing."

"Definitely," Gere agreed, completely missing the irony in the remark.

KEVIN, ALREADY WIRED over the impending carnival, reacted with the anticipated enthusiasm over seeing where the bug doctor worked. "Does this dude really have a lot of bugs?" he asked Shelley, even as he buckled the seat belt on the passenger side of her Jeep.

"This 'dude' is a doctor twice over, Kevin," Shelley said. "Please don't forget to call him that."

"Dr. Bug!" Kevin exclaimed, then laughed at Shelley's outrage when she corrected him, saying Gere's last name quite distinctly. Then, unexpectedly, he asked, "Are you scared of this dude, or something?"

"Scared of him?" Shelley echoed. "Where'd you get a ridiculous idea like that?"

"You just seem kind of S-Oed—stressed out." He mimicked her: "We have to be polite. We have to call him doctor."

"Brat!" Shelley countered affectionately. "S-Oed, indeed! I just want you to appreciate how special it is to be getting a personal guided tour of a research institute. Good manners never—"

"Go out of style," Kevin finished petulantly, with an impatient sigh. "I know. Don't worry. I'll be C-O."

"Somehow I don't think you mean commanding officer," Shelley said, sending Kevin into a fit of arrogant adolescent laughter.

"C-O means chilled out," he explained after recovering.

"Well," Shelley said, "I guess a person's *never* too old to learn, are they?"

"Guess not," Kevin responded, with an earnestness that made her want to tell him to go wash behind his ears again. He was growing up so fast. So fast. Where was the baby she'd rocked to sleep so many times?

He's C-O! she answered herself wryly. He'd already sensed her tension where Gere was concerned. She could only hope he wasn't C-O enough to pick up on the sexual tension between her and Gere.

"This guy sure lives out in the sticks, doesn't he?" Kevin observed, when Shelley left the highway and turned onto a winding country road.

She laughed at Kevin's city-boy perspective. "He has to be where the bugs are."

Gere had left the gate open for them, so she parked in the driveway. The Dalmatians dashed around from the backyard to greet them as they exited the Jeep, delighting Kevin, who knelt to pet them and let them lick his face. "Dalmatians! Just like in the movie! What are their names?"

"Wigglesworth and von Frisch," Shelley said, grinning at Gere, who was approaching from the rear of the house.

"Weird names," Kevin remarked. "Which is which?"

Shelley shrugged and raised her eyebrows at Gere. "I can't tell them apart. Perhaps you'd better ask Dr. Booth."

Kevin noticed Gere for the first time and straightened, filling Shelley with pride as he shook Gere's hand in a very adult way when she made introductions, and addressed him as Dr. Booth.

They talked for a bit about the dogs, Gere telling him that Wigglesworth was an insect physiologist, and then explaining, in simple language but without condescension, that a physiologist studies how bodies are put together and how they function.

Kevin, fair like Shelley, and slightly chubby, listened attentively, then asked, "And what about von Frisch? Was he a physiologist, too?"

"Inquiring minds want to know," Shelley murmured to Gere, giving him a smile of encouragement over her brother's head. Then, looking at Kevin, she said, "Von Frisch discovered the honeybee dance patterns."

"What's that?"

Gere explained while leading them across the backyard. "It's the way bees tell each other where to find flowers. You see, one bee finds a great patch of flowers, and when he carries the pollen back to the hive for the other worker bees to make honey from it, he does a dance, and the other bees know from the way he dances which way they should fly to find flowers. It's like giving directions."

"No!" Kevin said, obviously enchanted by the idea.

"Sure. Sort of like the way baseball players send each other messages when they tip their caps or scratch their noses. Or like the referees at football games make their calls with hand signals."

"No!" Kevin said again, *loving* the idea.

Gere drew confidence from the boy's enthusiastic response. "Oh, yes," he assured him. "Scientists have made movies of bees inside a hive. And some scientists in Europe went even further. They made a robot bee and programmed it to dance different ways. Then they watched to see if the bees went where he'd told them to, and the bees did."

"Awesome!" Kevin exclaimed.

"I thought the same thing the first time I heard about it." Gere said nostalgically. He'd expected to be edgy and ill at ease, but Kevin's youthful enthusiasm made it easy to relax. Turning to face Kevin, he noted the boy's resemblance to Shelley. He also caught a glimpse of himself at the same age—curious and open-minded—and felt an unexpected wave of tenderness for the child. "I understand you want to learn all about being an entomologist."

"Yes, sir," Kevin said, then amended, "Dr. Booth."

"Well, here's the best thing about the job," Gere told him, extending his arm toward the wooded area beyond the lawn. "This is my field laboratory. Want to go do some research?"

"Sure!" Kevin replied.

Shelley, who'd deliberately slowed her gait to let Gere and Kevin walk ahead of her, grinned with satisfaction as the two, with Wigglesworth and von Frisch at their heels, followed a crude path into the foliage. *And Gere had worried that he wouldn't know how to relate to a child. He had Kevin drooling over the prospect of becoming an entomologist.*

She hung back a ways, watching and listening as Gere pulled aside leaves to show Kevin evidence of insects at some stage of development. They examined ants crawling on a log, beetles and roly-polies in the bleached area under the log, something burrowed in the bark of a pine tree, with Gere constantly supplying fascinating tidbits of information about the insects he exposed.

"So, what do you think of my field laboratory?" Gere asked finally.

"Awesome," Kevin said.

"Ready to take a look at my indoor laboratory? I've got some experiments in progress you might be interested in."

"Do you have any robot bees?" Kevin asked hopefully.

Gere laughed. "I'm afraid not. I've never done any honeybee research. I have some moths just coming out of their cocoons, though."

"I want to see the frogs," Kevin said.

"The frogs it is, then," Gere agreed, and beamed a relieved smile at Shelley over the boy's head. Shelley nodded subtly, acknowledging that everything was going splendidly.

The frogs drew the anticipated enthusiasm, and Kevin spent several minutes going over the detailed records of what insects had been released into their tanks on which days. Finally he hung the clipboard back on the hook with a somber shake of his head. "Entomologists sure have to write a lot, don't they?"

"Meticulous record keeping is essential to any kind of scientific observation," Gere told him, then, with a conspiratorial wink, added, "It's not my favorite part of the job, either. I'd much rather deal with the insects."

The moths were next on the tour. "I've had these guys since they were caterpillars, letting half of them feed on one type of plant, and the other half feed on another. See how I've marked the wings of the hatchlings so I'll know which is which?"

"These are the ones you're setting free at night?" Shelley asked, pinning Gere with a significant "look."

"At dusk, actually," Gere corrected. "Of course, I have to observe them for some time afterward."

Shelley glared disparagingly at the innocent-looking moths in the same way many women would scowl at a set of golf clubs. She was being unreasonable, of course. Unreasonable, selfish, possessive, petty and paranoid. But she couldn't shake the feeling that watching moths was as much an *excuse* not to be with her as it was a *reason* that he couldn't be with her.

Call it instinct, women's intuition, cosmic vibrations or psychic divination, she *knew* when a man was deliberately avoiding her. What she couldn't figure out was why *this* man was.

He never looked at her without a glint of desire in his eyes, and she never met his heated gaze without an awareness of the explosive sexual attraction arcing between them. It was impossible for her to believe, as his gaze met hers above Kevin's head, that Gere's ardor was cooling. Even the lenses of his heavy-framed eyeglasses couldn't conceal the fire lurking in the depths of his green eyes. Whatever was going on inside that brilliant mind of his, the rest of him was still yearning for her.

Unless she was seeing what she wanted to see because she so desperately wanted to see it.

Unless she was believing what she wanted to believe because she wanted so badly to believe it.

Unless the fact that she'd fallen madly, head over heels in love with the incredible Dr. Hunk was letting hope blind her to reality.

It was a circle, a riddle, and she was no closer to an answer by the time Gere finished showing Kevin around the lab than she had been when she'd arrived. She was just a bit more deeply in love with this strange, unreadable man who could explain science to a child with infinite patience, and who'd had the foresight and thoughtfulness to buy that child a book about insects to carry home with him.

She interrupted Kevin's gushing speech of gratitude to suggest that he go outside and tell the Dalmatians goodbye while she talked to the doctor for a moment. She was in Gere's arms almost before the door closed behind her brother. The sigh of relief he exhaled as he wrapped his arms around her only reinforced her conviction that whatever his reason for avoiding her, it wasn't that he'd lost his desire for her.

"Are you sure you won't change your mind and go to the carnival with us?" she asked, as he walked with her and Kevin to the Jeep.

"It's going to be awesome," Kevin said. "They're having a moonwalk, and one of those things where you throw a baseball and somebody falls in the water, and our *principal* is going to get dunked. And we're going to throw pies at our teachers."

"That sounds like lots of fun," Gere answered vaguely.

"You could follow in the VW in case you need to leave earlier than we do," Shelley interjected.

She derived some pleasure from Gere's obvious discomfort as he searched for an excuse to replace the one she'd just stripped away.

"I have some errands to do this afternoon," he said, his grim expression ending any hope of his joining them.

Shelley shrugged resolutely. "Then you're just going to have to miss all the fun, Dr. Booth."

"Dunk the principal once for me!" Gere called after them as Shelley backed out of the drive, then laughed as Kevin shot him a thumbs-up sign.

The Jeep was hardly off his driveway and heading up the road before melancholy descended over him like a shroud. Shelley wouldn't be in his arms that night—and he had no one to blame but himself.

10

SPENDING TWO HOURS spraying whipped cream into foil
pie pans in the pie-throwing booth didn't do much for
Shelley's disposition, but if she had to spend two hours
up to her elbows in sticky cream, this was a good afternoon for it. As frustrated as she was over Gere's peculiar behavior, she could hardly be any more
miserable in the pie booth than anywhere else on the
planet Earth.

She might not be a mathematician, but she was sharp
enough to know when something didn't add up. And
the "something" that didn't add up was the cold water
that Dr. Garrick Booth was dumping on their relationship all of a sudden.

Okay, so he had this thing about saving the world
through naturally-occurring chemicals, and he had to
go out and help his male moths score with some females in order to do it. So he had to be where the female moths were, when the female moths were in a
receptive mood. That left a lot of weekend hours un-
accounted for—hours he could spend with a human
female who was in a receptive mood.

*If he wanted to spend hours with a certain receptive
human of the female persuasion, that was.* And unless
she was mistaken by a mile, unless his kiss this morning had been a lie, he was definitely receptive to the female in question. That brought her back to the same
vexing question she'd been wrestling with since he'd

told her he wouldn't have time to be with her this weekend: Why wasn't he making the effort?

Wasn't their relationship important enough to him to make the effort? Or, maybe she wasn't the only receptive female flapping around the good doctor.

Every fiber of her being wanted to reject both possibilities. She was too head over heels to accept that the relationship meant any less to him than to her. And the idea of Dr. Garrick "I've-only-made-love-to-one-woman-in-my-entire-life" Booth juggling two women at once was just too ludicrous.

Unless his kisses were lies.

Unless her instincts were totally malfunctioning.

Unless she'd fallen—hook, line and sinker—for one of the most elaborate absentminded-professor-awakened scams ever perpetrated against a gullible female.

What did she know about him, anyway? She'd never have noticed him if he hadn't been getting letters addressed to Dr. Hunk. She could be the biggest fool that had ever been born. He'd gone from absentminded professor to dance-floor dynamo in an incredibly short time. For all she knew, he could be the Don Juan of the worldwide scientific community. He might be known in the farthermost reaches of the globe as Dr. Hunk, grand master of chemical sexual attractants. He might take a different woman to Gaspard's every Saturday night. He might be the rumba king of Boston. Hell, he could be the U.S. national lambada champion!

Or he could be the sweetest, noblest man and most dedicated scientist in the whole wide world. He could be in his lab working, alone and lonely, facing a long and lonelier night. And she could be the luckiest woman on the face of the earth to have discovered him.

She rather liked the second set of possibilities, the ones contingent upon Gere being exactly what he seemed to be, and as madly in love with her as she was with him. But no matter what the situation was, she had to find out *what* the situation was. She was not a woman who stood idly by and let things happen; she was a woman who took the offensive and *made* things happen.

She planned her strategy while absently spewing cream into an endless parade of pie pans. She was about to take the bull—or rather, the entomologist—by the horns, or the antennae, or some other convenient part of his scientist's physiology and find out exactly where she stood with the incredible Dr. Hunk!

A shower, a shampoo, a change into fresh clothes and an hour's preening in the mirror later, she parked her Jeep in front of Gere's mailbox. Since he wasn't expecting her, the gates were closed and padlocked. Von Frisch and Wigglesworth arrived to lick her ankles by the time she'd climbed the fence, gingerly juggling her purse and the bag of carnival goodies she'd brought along, and was easing herself down on the inside.

She could have honked and waited for Gere to come out and let her in, but she liked having the element of surprise on her side. Either she was going to find Gere playing matchmaker to a flock—or should it be swarm?—of horny moths, or she was going to find him otherwise engaged.

She hadn't realized, until she squared her shoulders in resolve and started up the drive toward the clearing out back, how fiercely she wanted to find him in his field laboratory, playing matchmaker to a flock—or should it be swarm?—of horny moths. She hadn't realized, until she spied him, totally engrossed in his work and oblivious to her presence, how solitary his work must be at times.

He was wearing old jeans, his tattered Harvard shirt, hiking boots, and a miner's hat with a lantern mounted on it. She followed the beam from the lantern to a patch of weeds he appeared to be observing and stood perfectly still as Gere opened the lid of a screened cage and urged a male moth to freedom.

With breathless anticipation, she watched the moth flutter, get his bearings and fly in the direction of the weeds. Anticipation turned to fascination as the freed male seemed to select a specific plant and hovered above it. Then Shelley spotted another moth sitting on the weed. Noticing the male, the female grew restless and quivered, and even to an untrained observer, it was obvious that some type of negotiation was going on. Suddenly the female capitulated, and the two moths came together. Coupled, they flitted closely together, their wings overlapping.

Shelley was too awed to move. Still unaware of her presence, Gere approached the weed and tenderly scooped the mating pair into his hands. As he turned to carry the two moths to one of his screened cages, the beam from his lantern swept past Shelley. He froze, then jerked his head back for a double take, as if to verify what he'd seen.

"I could have been the maniac with the hook," she said wryly.

"Shelley?"

She squinted under the blinding glare of the lantern when the beam hit her straight on. "Sorry," he said, twisting his head to the side. He took a step toward her, then remembered the moths he was holding and detoured to deposit them in the proper cage with meticulous care before turning back to her.

"Close your eyes," he said, putting his hands on her shoulders.

"What?"

"The light . . . I can't keep my head turned sideways for long or I'll get a crick in my neck."

Eyes closed, Shelley heard the whisper of his approach, sensed the light and his gaze on her face, felt the warmth emanating from his body as he stood in front of her. "I'll leave if I'm interrupting your work," she said.

He took an unforgivably long time before answering, on the tail end of a long exhalation. "God, you're beautiful."

His fingertips were gentle as they swept over her cheeks, brushed over her mouth, and cupped her chin, urging her head back. She felt his body tremble with the effort of control as his lips lighted on hers.

Suddenly they were kissing, clinging desperately to each other. Memories, tactile as well as mental, of the hours they'd spent making love swept over them, igniting need and passion. Shelley pulled her mouth from his to kiss his cheek, his jawline, his neck. "Does this mean you're glad to see me?"

"If I was any gladder to see you, you'd have the imprint of twigs and pebbles on your backside."

She nestled her cheek against his chest, listening to his heart. "Do you want me to leave?"

"Not in this century."

"Can I help with your work?"

"You can watch. I'm almost finished out here."

"I'm not fouling anything up, am I? I mean, with my scent?"

"Only my concentration," he said wryly. "The moths are too busy smelling each other to notice either of us."

"The ones you picked up earlier didn't try to fly away."

"When they're mating, they're in sort of a stupor. They probably weren't even aware of my presence."

Shelley lifted her head from his chest. "You mean they were still mating?"

"They will be for several hours."

"For hours?"

"Mmm-hmm."

"How marvelous for them."

The innuendo in the wistful comment shot through Gere like molten lava. He remembered too well the sweetness of making love to her not to appreciate the prospect of spending hours doing so. That she should feel comfortable enough with him to let him know she would enjoy making love for hours filled him with pride. And hope. And expectation.

"If I kiss you again, I won't finish my work, and you'll have the imprint of twigs and pebbles on your back-side."

"Promises, promises," Shelley teased.

"Another time," he promised. "We'll bring a blanket and a bottle of wine."

Shelley grinned. "Sounds like seduction, entomologist's-style, to me."

"I may have heard one or two colleagues discussing . . . interesting field encounters," Gere confessed.

Laughing, Shelley hooked her arm through his as they walked toward his field gear. "So, tell me about the encounters your moths are having."

He released another male and explained what was happening. "See how active the females are becoming?

They have released their pheromone, any second, now . . . Yes. There he goes. See how he's interested in a particular female?"

Shelley nodded.

"He's following her scent. Obviously he likes what she's offering. Now he'll be giving her a whiff of what he's offering to see if she's interested."

"How does she let him know if she is?"

"She curls her abdomen in the air."

Shelley studied his face for signs that he was teasing her, but he was deadly serious.

"It's 'Hey, baby, you want to do it?' then a simple yes or no, huh?"

Gere grinned. "They're a lot more direct than humans. It's probably because their entire reason for existence is to reproduce. They don't have time for games."

"I thought they had to wreak havoc in closets and rugs somewhere along the way."

"You're thinking of the gypsy moth. These guys aren't a nuisance to anyone."

"Oh, look, Gere!" The moths had coupled, and were soaring toward the weeds. "She must have raised her tail."

"She must have," Gere agreed, keeping the light trained on the pair while he walked over to collect them.

He released two more males, both of whom found partners. "If I had this success rate at singles bars, I might go out more often," Gere said, obviously pleased with the evening's work as he packed up his gear.

"You probably do all right," Shelley muttered under her breath, not expecting him to hear.

Gere stopped what he was doing. "You don't get it, do you? Shelley, I'm not the man you think I am."

"I don't—"

"I've *never* been to a singles bar!" he said. "Unless you count the time that they threw Heath's bachelor party in the private back room of a local club so they could have a stripper come in and dance to 'Get Me to the Church on Time.'"

The heart-to-mush converter had done it again. The urge to tell him she loved him was so strong, Shelley had to clamp her jaw shut to keep from succumbing to it. She had already risked her pride, showing up uninvited; she wasn't going to push her luck. No matter how fast or how far she had to chase him, she was just old-fashioned enough to want to hear it from him first.

"What's in the bag?" he asked, noticing her shopping bag for the first time as he put down his own gear in the lab.

"Carnival loot," she replied. "I felt sorry for you, stuck here while I was out having fun, so I thought we might have a do-it-yourself carnival. Mind if I stash something in the fridge?"

"A surprise?"

"You could say that."

"Through that door and to the left," Gere said, indicating a sliding-glass patio door that led into the main house.

He was gingerly transferring the coupled moths into a large screened enclosure when she returned from the kitchen. "What now?"

"We leave them alone in their ecstasy. The females will lay their eggs, and I'll release the adults. Then we'll see how this group of hatchlings fares in comparison to the control group."

"Control group?"

"The offspring of the males raised on a standard diet."

"You mean these males—"

"Were the ones raised on a special diet of beans that are toxic to most other insects. The theory is that the toxin from the beans shows up in the male's phero- mone and the female moth chooses him in part be- cause she knows that his—we'll say *juices* for want of a better word—will help protect her offspring from predators. We've already got a strong indication that these little fellows are popular with the ladies. If their offspring prove to have a higher survival rate, then that will add strength to the 'survival selection' theory."

Listening to him speak so animatedly about his work, Shelley resigned herself to a future with a heart of pure mush. "So you're finished for the night?" she asked suggestively, slipping her hands over his shoulders.

"With the moths," he said, enchanted by the sensa- tions created by her teeth on his earlobe.

"How would you like to come to a carnival with me?" she whispered.

"I'd go to the moon and back with you if you asked me like that," he replied. "Which reminds me—"

"Reminds you of what?" she asked, drawing away from his kiss a long time later.

"I have a surprise for you, too. Come on." He led her into the house, through the breakfast nook, to another patio door. "Close your eyes."

"Do you use that line with all the women, or just with me?"

"You trust me, don't you? I won't steer you into any walls."

They didn't walk far before he stopped and positioned her just so, by putting his hands on her shoulders. "You can open your eyes now."

Shelley couldn't *believe* her eyes. "It's a hammock!"

"For two," Gere said. "The next best thing to playground equipment. We'll have the stars and the moon just beyond the screen roof, but we won't be bothered by any cops."

"There's still the maniac with the hook."

Gere shook his head. "The dogs would alert us."

"The way they alerted you to me?"

"They know you. How'd you get inside the fence, anyway?"

"Climbed over."

"You should have honked."

"I didn't want to disturb you. Besides, I wanted to make sure you weren't with some leggy redhead." She gave the hammock a gentle shove, setting it rocking. "I can't believe you bought a hammock just for—"

"I'm developing a lecherous streak," he said wryly. "I was hoping you'd help me with it."

Shelley flung herself onto the hammock and held out her arms beseechingly. "I'd love to, Doc."

Gere sat down next to her. The hammock pitched and he suddenly found himself seated inelegantly on the floor. Shelley rolled onto her side so that they were eye to eye, and giggled. "Well, it was good for me. How was it for you?"

Frowning, Gere stood, unconsciously rubbing his bruised rump. *Some lecher—he couldn't even climb into a hammock!* "Move over," he ordered grumpily. "Closer to the edge."

"I'll fall off the other side," she protested.

"No, you won't. We're going to do this scientifically. I'll counterbalance with my hand at first, and then my weight will balance it when I stretch out."

"If I land on my keister, I'll show *you* the scientific approach!" Shelley threatened.

"See? It worked!" Gere told her, when they were stretched out, side by side.

"I'll say it did!" Shelley said, as gravity exerted itself and the net bed of the hammock wedged them together, full length and face-to-face. Caressing Gere's cheek in her palm, she kissed him briefly on the lips and sighed. "Didn't you say something about helping you with a lecherous streak?"

He shifted his arm so that her neck was cradled by his shoulder. "You're giving it all the encouragement it needs at the moment."

"Oh? And I was going to let you smell my wrist."

"Your wrist?"

She held it just beneath his nose beguilingly. "My perfume. It's the closest I can come to a pheromone. Do you like it?"

"Hmm."

"I'll take it that means yes."

"Hmm," Gere confirmed.

"I hope this means I get to sample yours."

Through a haze of sexual arousal, Gere remembered the cologne his sister had given him—the one he hadn't worn since last Saturday night. "I didn't put any on. I wasn't planning—"

Shelley laughed—a rich, throaty and slightly ribald chuckle. "I'm sure a genius like you can think of some way to find out if a woman's . . . receptive."

Gere wasn't *thinking* straight about anything. For once, he followed his instincts without thinking, tightening his arms around her and fusing his mouth over hers, mindlessly succumbing to the pleasure of being close enough to touch her.

After an eternity of sensation, Shelley raised her head, breaking the kiss, and asked breathlessly, "What was it you said the female moth does to indicate she's interested?"

"She curls up her abdomen?" he said, as though not entirely sure.

"Like this?"

Gere gasped as she pressed her pelvis into his. He was instantly hard and instantly hot, consumed by his burning need to possess her. And Shelley knew it. "If you were a lightning bug, you'd be glowing," she taunted.

Desperate for more, he responded by cupping her buttocks in his hands and pulling her closer, anchoring her against him while the heat from their bodies blended into an inferno of desire that consumed them both.

As desperate as Gere, Shelley responded with a fervor and energy that made the term "receptive" totally inadequate. She made love to him with a mesmerizing blend of tenderness and urgent longing, ripping at his clothes and at her own, proving with her mouth, her hands, her entire body that she needed him as much as he needed her. Her skin was heated and damp, her hands greedy, questing and ingenious as she touched him, stroking, kneading, urgently grasping.

The hammock became an erotic cradle of love, rocking with their every movement, while its net bed tightened around them, pressing them harder together. Moonlight filtered through the screen roof to bathe them in an enchanted glow.

Every sound, every movement Shelley made incited Gere; each caress, each whispered entreaty, each urgent whimper of appreciation stoked his frenzied need of her. When she convulsed against him in a spasm of fulfillment and called out his name as though he had the capacity to conquer every fear and solve every problem she'd ever had or ever could have, he answered with her name and thrust into her in the throes of his own devastating, terrifying, splendid release that left him more stuporous than his moths.

They lay there, too replete to move, or to think, for a long time before Shelley said, "Gere?"

"Hmm?"

"Was there an earthquake?"

"We'll read the newspaper in the morning and find out."

A silence ensued.

Tell me you love me, Shelley thought fiercely. *I feel it, but I need to hear it, just once.*

Gere wasn't thinking. He was doing everything he could *not* to think. The intensity of their lovemaking left him too exhausted and confused for thinking. He was afraid to speak, for fear of saying too much. Or not enough. Or the *wrong* thing. His mind was uncommonly muddled. He wasn't accustomed to this degree of emotional intensity, loss of control, vulnerability. What he wished for more than anything else in the world was a solitary moment to collect and sort the thoughts and feelings churning through his mind, heart and soul.

Could she really read his mind? he wondered, when Shelley provided him the perfect opportunity. Pushing up on an elbow—no mean feat in that net bed—she said, "Mind if I borrow your shirt?" When he just blinked at her uncomprehendingly, she said, "If the Harvard seal is sacred, I'll understand. It's just that it's longer than mine, and I'd kind of like to find your bathroom."

"Go ahead," he said, finally.

Shelley rolled out of the hammock and pulled the shirt on. Soft with age and wear, it molded over the curves of her body, the Harvard seal clinging to her breasts.

"You do the old school proud," Gere observed.

Shelley smoothed her palms over the front of the shirt and looked unflinchingly into his eyes. "It's almost like having you touch me."

Gere turned away from the intimacy of her gaze. "There's a bathroom at the end of the hall."

He waited until he heard the door close before going to the bathroom in the master suite. He'd regained his emotional equilibrium by the time he'd taken a shower and put on fresh clothes—enough equilibrium, at least, to remember to slap on some of the cologne Kelsey had given him and pull the sheets on the unmade bed into order.

He was whistling to himself as he rounded the corner into the living room, and was caught totally off guard when he was attacked by a giant squawking bird.

"Gotcha!" Shelley cried, when he leaped back, instinctively raising his arms to shield his face and swearing like a sailor.

He repeated one of the choice curses when he realized the "bird" he was fending off was actually a blowout snake whistle with a feather at the end.

"Welcome to the carnival!" she said, laughing. She grabbed his hand with such affection that he couldn't have been angry with her if he'd wanted to be. "Come on. I have all kinds of stuff."

"I can hardly wait," Gere grumbled, a willing captive to her fun despite his grumpiness. They went back to the hammock, this time sitting Indian-style, facing each other. Shelley treated her "carnival" bag like a Santa's sack, drawing out one curiosity at a time—straw finger traps, which Gere pretended not to know how to get out of; a puzzle you tilted back and forth, trying to get black balls to stay in depressions in a cardboard picture of a Dalmatian, thus putting "spots" on the dog; a cheap kazoo on which she goaded Gere into humming the Harvard alma mater.

"And now—" she announced, poking her hand deeply into the bag. "Ta-da! I saved the best for last."

"Cotton candy?"

She seemed offended by his consternation. "It's the best thing about any carnival!"

She gingerly removed the plastic covering from the wad of pink candy, then tapped his lips with the spun sugar. "How long has it been since you had cotton candy?"

"I can't even remember."

"Well, that's too long. Come on. Take a bite. It'll sweeten your disposition."

She waited for him to comply, then tore a strip from the opposite side of the candy wad at the same time. "You know what they say about people sharing cotton candy."

"What?"

"It spreads germs," she said impishly. "Good, huh?"

"Too sweet!" Gere protested, scrunching up his nose.

Shelley suddenly grew pensive. "You were good with Kevin this morning. He was very impressed."

"He's a bright kid."

"He told his science teacher all about his tour. She asked if the institute gave group tours."

"Eventually I hope to establish a public education program."

"PR for bugs?" She tore a long strip from the candy and ate it.

"Sort of."

"Tonight...the moths... It was fascinating they way they came together. There was a sort of...natural beauty about it. I think I got a glimpse of what draws you to this work." She tore off another strip of sugar, but stopped before putting it in her mouth. "I'm being serious, and you're grinning."

"It wasn't what you're saying, it's the candy. It looks like silk."

She cast a doubting glance at the candy. "Silk?"

"Insect silk. Like silkworms and spiders produce. Some flies produce it, too."

"Sorry to disappoint you, but I didn't spin this myself."

"If we were flies," Gere told her, "I would be the one doing the spinning. I would have caught the juiciest bug I could find and wrapped it in silk in order to lure you to me."

"And if I were a fly, I guess I'd be impressed."

"Undoubtedly. You see, some species of flies don't eat much once they're adults, and you'd be on the lookout for some male fly with a big, silk-wrapped bug so you could eat it and have enough strength for laying your eggs after you'd mated."

"The insect version of 'Show me your portfolio'?"

He laughed. "I'm going to have to start writing down all your insect-to-human analogies for when we establish that educational program."

"What about the poor male flies who aren't good hunters—do they do without?"

"Not," Gere said dramatically, "if they're clever. If they're clever enough, they just spin a lot of silk and make a big bundle to make the female think there's a juicy bug inside."

"Wouldn't she fly away when she discovered he'd lied?"

"By that time, it would probably be too late. The female feeds while they're mating. The male does all the work. By the time she gets inside the silk, she could already be deflowered."

Shelley's eyes were wide as saucers. "She eats . . . *during?*"

"It's terribly humiliating for the male fly," Gere said.

"Not to mention the poor deflowered virgins who don't have enough strength to lay their eggs." She shoved the cotton candy back into the plastic wrapper, then asked thoughtfully, "Where would I have to go to take a class on insects?"

"A class?"

"Yes. If I wanted to learn about insects, where would I take a class?"

Gere considered the question a minute. "You'd need a four-year school for the specific entomology classes. The University of Florida has a good school, but I wouldn't want you going there."

"Why not?"

"Because you'd have to move to Gainesville, and I'd miss you."

"You would?" she asked, grinning from ear to ear.

"Does that surprise you?"

"Not exactly. But a lady likes to hear the words sometimes."

"I'm not particularly articulate in that arena."

"You do all right," she said, suddenly self-conscious.

They fell silent a moment, then, abruptly, Gere asked, "Why are you here, Shelley?"

"I told you. I felt bad about your having to miss all the— Oh, hell!" Her shoulders sagged, as she realized nothing would ring true but the truth. "Isn't it obvious, Gere? I'm here because I missed you. I wanted to be with you. I was hurt when you told me you didn't have time for me, and I had to find out. . . ."

Her voice tapered into a miserable silence. "Find out what?" Gere asked, almost afraid to hear.

"Find out *why,* after last weekend, you weren't making time for us."

"I explained about that. The moths—"

"If you'd wanted to be with me enough, you could have found a way. We did. Tonight. You could have gone to the carnival."

"I had to pick up the hammock this afternoon."

Pick up the hammock. It was enough to make a grown woman cry. Shelley choked down the sob in her throat and blinked back the unshed tears burning her eyes.

Gere had a sense of things going terribly awry. Shelley looked so hurt and vulnerable. His insides wrenched at the thought that he might be responsible for the wounded expression on Shelley's face. He swallowed a lump that had formed in his throat, wishing he knew how to soothe her. Guilt was one accursed emotion, particularly when a man didn't know what he was guilty of.

Her chin quivered. She thrust it bravely upward and said, "Just tell me one thing, Gere. Were you planning on asking me to try it out with you?"

If Gere lived to be a thousand, he'd never understand women. "Why do you *think* I bought it?"

"*Why* you bought it is obvious. The question is, was it a one-woman hammock?"

Nothing could have surprised him more. "You think—?"

"What was I supposed to think when you suddenly didn't have time for me?"

"That I was terrified!" Gere hadn't meant to confess it, much less shout it out for her and the whole world to hear.

"Of me?" Shelley asked, her consternation reflecting the same confusion he felt.

"Of you. Of the things you made me want and made me feel. Of the things my feelings for you forced me to think about."

Her eyes searched his face. "What *things*, Gere?"

"The future," he said. "Children. Did you think I didn't see the expression on your face when your friend announced she was going to have a baby? Or hear the yearning in your voice when you talk about your baby brother? You want children, and I've never given having children a moment's thought."

"You were thinking about having children with me?"

This time she looked as if she really might cry. Gere didn't know what he would do if that happened.

"You don't have to push me away, Gere. We don't have to rush into anything."

"Push you away?" His eyes searched her troubled face. "Do you think I would ever have the strength or the will to push you away?"

"But you didn't want to see me this weekend."

"You think I didn't want to be with you? You think I didn't want to make love with you again?" He cradled her face in his hands. "I was missing you when I was driving home from your house Sunday night. I just didn't want to be with you when I wasn't—"

He released a sigh of frustration. "I'm not always the hunk you went out with last weekend—the cool guy with the fancy clothes. The one you made love to."

Shelley jerked away from his touch as though he'd struck her, and fixed his face with a murderous glare. "The man I made love to was the man who went to the library and checked out videos so he could dance with me. He's the man who was in that playground with me, looking at the stars. He's the man who regaled my baby brother with stories about robot honeybees. I thought *that* was who was in the hammock with me about an hour ago. Was I mistaken?"

Gere closed his eyes and exhaled deeply. "I've been incredibly stupid, haven't I?"

Shelley was in no frame of mind to disabuse him of the notion.

"I've been going through hell," he said, "afraid you were going to discover I wasn't that other guy. The cool one. The one you said making love to was like a dream. So afraid you'd wake up from the dream and quit—"

"Quit what?" she prompted softly.

"Quit wanting me. Quit making love to me."

"Because you weren't in your party clothes, with your hair spiked up? Because you weren't wearing high-top basketball shoes? Does that mean you only want to make love to me when I'm all dressed up to party, with my denim miniskirt and that little knit shirt with the buttons down the front?"

"What it means," Gere said, cupping her chin with his fingertips and tilting her face so that she was forced to look at him, "is that I'm inexperienced and insecure when it comes to relationships with women."

And does the way you're looking at me mean you love me? Shelley wondered fiercely. She waited, hoping, willing him to say it. But when he finally spoke, what he said was, "Have I messed everything up?"

Smiling, Shelley leaned forward to put her hands on his shoulders. "Kiss me and we'll find out."

Gere meant to keep it simple, gentle, but as always, the taste of her roused a hunger in him that wasn't easily sated. The briefest brush of his lips over hers led to more—a deeper kiss—and he wrapped his arms around her neck and lay back, straightening his legs and pulling her on top of him. The hammock compressed around them, cocooning them. Shelley's lips parted, and he probed the depths of her mouth, drunk with the heady sensation the taste of her evoked in him.

"Well?" he said, after ending the kiss.

"I think we just weathered our first crisis," she replied, in words soft as sighs.

They lay there, still and content. Then, suddenly, Shelley pushed up on her arms and looked down at Gere's face. "I just remembered something—the last surprise from the carnival."

"The one in the fridge."

"Mmm-hmm. I think now's the perfect time for it."

"I was just thinking that now would be a perfect time for you to kiss me again."

"Greedy man," she teased. "If I kiss you anymore, my lips are going to fall off. No, it's definitely time for the surprise."

"I hope it's ice cream," Gere said, as she gingerly climbed out of the hammock. And then, unexpectedly, he grinned lasciviously. "God, I love that shirt."

Shelley looked down and discovered that the front of the shirt was so askew that her breasts were easily revealed by the armholes Gere had enlarged when he'd cut out the sleeves. Pulling it aright, she snapped, "It's not ice cream. So there."

She was gone for what seemed to him to be a long time before she called out, "Sit up, and close your eyes. No fair peeking."

"I may be stupid sometimes, but I'm always honorable," he said.

"You can look now." She was standing directly in front of him. "See? It isn't ice cream."

"A pie!" he said, trying to sound enthusiastic. "What kind is it?"

"It's In-Your-Face Pie!" she answered, hitting him dead-on. "And that's for thinking I made love to you because of your fancy clothes!"

Sputtering and gasping, Gere wiped the chilled whipped cream away from his eye's with his fingertips. The cold, sticky cream hung from his skin in grotesque dollops and dripped from his eyebrows, and the golden piecrust stuck to the cream in messy globs.

Shelley giggled. He looked so ridiculous, so absurd, so outraged. His eyes glowed with a homicidal impulse as he glared back at her.

Swallowing her mirth, Shelly took an involuntary step backward. He was so large, so strong, so...angry.

"Gere?" she pleaded weakly. "You, uh, do have a sense of humor, don't you?"

There was only a horrid silence. And that murderous scowl.

"Say something, Gere. Talk to me. It was only a joke." She tried to laugh, then turned serious again. "If you're angry, we can work this out. Just tell me what you're thinking."

"I think," he said dramatically, scraping a wide streak of the cream from his cheek and smearing it across hers, "that we're about to weather our second crisis."

11

GERE CALLED KELSEY after Shelley left. "She doesn't care that I'm not a hunk all the time," he said.

"What'd you do, Gere, just ask her point-blank?" Kelsey demanded, sounding surprised.

"It just sort of came up. It's amusing, actually. Rather ironic. She thought I didn't *want* to see her because I told her I *couldn't* see her because the moths were mating."

"Quick on the uptake, is she?"

"Don't be so sarcastic all the time! She thought maybe I had another woman. That's why she climbed the fence instead of honking."

"Your life has certainly taken an interesting turn since you met this woman."

Ignoring her sarcasm, Gere reported, "She agrees that we need to take things slow, because everything happened so fast, and we haven't known each other long enough to know each other all that well."

"She told you this after she climbed the fence?"

"Oh, much later. After we'd cleaned up the whipped cream." He grinned at the memory of it. If Kelsey only knew how interesting his life had become!

"Whipped cream?" Kelsey repeated, with a giggle. "You're not turning kinky on me, are you, Big Brother?"

"It was from the *pie*," Gere said indignantly.

"She baked you a pie?" Kelsey asked delightedly.

"No. She hit me in the face with one."

"Now, who's being sarcastic?"

Gere decided to ignore the gibe. "We had a long talk, and she's done as much thinking about how different we are as I have, but she's more worried about the Ph.D. thing than about our philosophical differences."

"The Ph.D. thing?"

"That I have two Ph.D.'s from Haa-vaad, and she doesn't have any degrees at all because she's a professional class junkie."

"Whoa!" Kelsey said. "Back up. Did I just hear my brother, Garrick Lloyd Booth, deliberately distort the pronunciation of his alma mater?"

"You should hear the way Shelley says it. She's adorable."

"I'm liking her more every minute." The sarcasm in Kelsey's voice was gone.

"You're going to love her," Gere said. "I do."

Kelsey was quiet for a long time. "Are you sure, Gere?"

"I get surer every minute."

"Have you told her?"

"Not exactly. But I think she knows. She's . . . intuitive."

"I believe *nuts* was the word you used the last time we talked."

"*Nuts* was a bit strong," Gere said.

"If I were you," Kelsey advised gravely, "I'd tell her how I felt. Women like to hear things like that. *Especially* if they're intuitive. They *need* to hear it."

"Kelsey?" Gere was very serious.

"What is it?"

"She says a dreamer can be practical, and even a scientist can learn to dream. And Kel—"

"Hmm?"

"She told me that she loves me."

Gere held his breath while he waited for his sister's reaction. After a thoughtful pause, Kelsey said, "I have a feeling that she's going to be very good for you."

"She already has been," Gere replied, grinning.

"Then I'd say you have some talking to do, Big Brother."

"Yes-s-s!" Gere agreed. He hadn't needed Kelsey to tell him what to do, but it felt good finally to allow himself to admit what he'd known all along: that he was in love with Shelley. He said his sister's name softly.

"Hmm?"

"Thanks. For...everything. I would have been alone in the woods if you hadn't helped me."

"What's a little sister for?"

Her voice sounded suspiciously liquid. "What's wrong?" Gere asked.

"Nothing. I'm just being a silly little sister."

"You're going to like her."

Kelsey sniffed. "I know. And she's going to make you very happy, and I'm going to be getting a sister, not losing a brother."

"Then what's wrong?"

"I'm just practicing for the wedding!" she said. "And I'm going to hang up before I really start bawling."

Hormonal influence, Gere thought. *Open-and-shut case!* Still, he took Kelsey's advice to heart. It was time to tell Shelley how he felt.

The next day, Monday, when Shelley pulled up to Gere's mailbox, he was waiting with a long-stemmed rose and a big kiss.

"I love you, too," he announced.

"Oh, Gere," Shelley said, feeling the burn of tears in her eyes. "Why do you have to tell me when I'm all hot and sticky and in the middle of my route?"

"Because I couldn't wait any longer."

"*Now* you get sentimental and impulsive!"

"Want to come over tonight and help me play Cupid with the moths?"

Shelley groaned as if in physical pain.

"What is it?"

"I didn't know you'd ask. Maggie and I are going to dinner." After an awkward silence, she suggested, "You could join us."

"Girls' Night Out? I don't think so. I couldn't get away until late, anyway."

There was another silence. "Maybe you could drop by on your way home. We could have—" he grinned wickedly "—pie or something."

"It would be awfully late."

"Maybe tomorrow night?"

"Maybe," Shelley said coquettishly, knowing that Gere knew as well as she that her "Maybe" meant "Yes, yes, yes!"

She was smiling as she drove away, and humming for the rest of the day. They were getting there. They were definitely getting there.

On Tuesday, Gere staked out a good vantage point from which he could watch Shelley's reaction when she saw what he'd left at the base of the mailbox post: a folded blanket, a picnic basket and a bottle of wine to which he'd taped a note that read, "Tonight."

He would never know how Shelley would have reacted, because it wasn't Shelley's Jeep that pulled up to the box. He raced to catch the substitute carrier before he drove away.

"Where's Shelley?" he demanded.

"Shelley?" The substitute carrier was painfully young, plain-looking but neatly groomed. Caught off guard by Gere's inquiry, he blurted out, "Shelley couldn't work today. Her Jeep was totaled last night."

"Totaled?"

"Yeah," said the young man, warming to the topic. "It must have been pretty bad. They brought in a chopper and everything."

Gere's heart leaped to his throat. "A chopper?"

"Yeah. A flying ambulance."

"Which hospital?"

"ORHS, I guess."

"ORHS?"

"Yeah. Orlando Regional. That's where most of the trauma cases go."

"Where is it?" Gere called over his shoulder. He was already dashing for the house. He had to get the dogs in, unlock the gate—

"Huh?"

"How do I get there?"

"It's in downtown Orlando. But—"

Gere made the trip in under half an hour, which had to be a record. All during the drive, he constantly repeated to himself, "She's going to be all right. She's got to be all right. She's going to be all right."

When he finally arrived at the hospital, his ordeal became even more frustrating. There was no Shelley Peters registered, but the woman at the front desk suggested that he might try the emergency and trauma center. Even with computerized registration, not everything got put into the computer right away in an emergency, especially at night.

He was forced to wait in line at the ER, only to learn there was no record of Shelley there, either. He was about ready to throw up his hands and try calling the post office when the admitting clerk spied an orderly. "Hey, Reggie? You worked last night, didn't you?"

"I sure did," Reggie said. "My tail's draggin' with these double shifts, too."

"Did the chopper bring in someone from a mail truck?"

"Whew. Yeah. Bad one."

"What happened?"

"They called in a surgeon. The family's up in the surgical waiting room."

Gere's thank-you was a blur of speech as he took off for the waiting area, realizing as he stepped into the crowded room that he'd never met any of Shelley's family except Kevin. "Does anyone here know Shelley Peters?" he called.

"Gere?"

Gere told himself his mind was playing tricks on him. He couldn't have heard her voice. He couldn't be seeing her. She was on an operating table, unconscious, while machines bleeped around her. She couldn't be walking toward him from a far corner of the room.

He quit fighting the idea when she wrapped her arms around him, clinging to him. "How did you—? Oh, Gere, I don't care how you got here, I'm just glad you are. It's so awful. Stanley's been in surgery for over eight hours. Barbara's a basket case. Maggie and I have been trying to keep her calm so she doesn't lose the baby. I don't think she could take that."

"Stanley?" Gere asked, dazed. He hadn't been letting himself feel, and now the relief hit him as hard as the fear he'd denied.

Shelley explained, "He had to work late, so Barbara went to dinner with us. Then his car blew a hose, and he borrowed the Jeep to see if he could find a replacement at a filling station. They don't know if he's going to make it."

"Your substitute told me your Jeep— I thought it was you," he said.

Her eyes widened. "You thought that I—?"

"At first, all I could see were images of you, hurt and bleeding. Then I thought, 'No. I won't let it happen.' So I kept making myself see you alive and well. I kept visualizing your smile."

"You visualized? While you were driving?"

"I didn't close my eyes but once, and I opened them when the pickup truck honked."

"Stanley Curtis?"

"That's the circulating nurse," Shelley said, taking Gere's hand and leading him to the nurse who'd just announced Stanley's name. "She's been out once before to give us an update. Oh, Gere, he had a rib through his lung, a lacerated liver and his spleen was ruptured. If he hadn't been wearing a seat belt, he'd have been killed instantly."

Barbara, braced by Maggie's arm, joined them, along with an older woman Gere assumed was Stan's mother. They all looked haggard and worn-out.

"He's out of surgery," the nurse said. "He'll be fine. The doctor was able to repair the liver, but they had to remove his spleen."

"His lung?" Barbara asked frantically.

"As I told you earlier, the doctor removed the bone chip that broke off his rib, and inflated the lung. I'll let him give you all the medical details, but barring unforeseen complications, Stanley should make a complete recovery."

Barbara, Maggie and the assembled relatives hugged en masse. Barbara was crying. "Stanley can be a jerk sometimes, but I couldn't imagine losing him."

"Thank God," Shelley murmured, clinging to Gere.

"I'm glad he's going to be all right," Gere said, then asked, "Do you feel like talking?"

Shelley nodded. "I'd just be in the way here. Maggie will fill me in on what the doctor says."

Gere led her to a corner of the room that was relatively uncrowded. "Kiss me."

All of the emotion of the past few hours filtered into the kiss. Shelley wondered how she'd ever let him go, but it wasn't a problem, because Gere showed no signs of wanting to go anywhere without her. Long after the kiss ended he clasped her tightly to him. She listened to his heartbeat, strong and reassuring and regular after so intimate a confrontation with the prospect of death.

"In times of crises," Gere said, stroking her hair, "everything comes more sharply into focus. Suddenly you know what's important, and everything else falls into perspective. I had one of those moments when I thought you were hurt. The one thing I knew was that I didn't want to lose you. Not ever. I don't have any more doubts, Shelley. We're on your timetable now. Whatever you're ready for. Whatever you want. Marriage. Kids. Just—"

He hugged her even tighter. "Don't ever leave me."

It was a proposal, she realized. Unorthodox, perhaps, but so was the man she'd fallen in love with.

"Does that smile mean yes?" he asked, his voice filled with hope and dread and love, and all the other emotions of a man in the process of making a lifelong commitment.

"I'm not even sure exactly what the question is," Shelley said. "But the answer's yes."

"I love your smile," he said, tracing her lips with his fingertip. "I love the rest of you, too, but your smile fills me up when I'm empty."

"It ought to," she said. "It's a magic smile—the smile that turned a frog into a prince."

"I thought that was supposed to be a kiss."

She remembered then. The first time he'd kissed her—on the playground. In the moonlight. Who'd have thought it? "I think it was a kiss that turned me into a princess," she said, raising her face to his. "Would you like to try for a goddess?"

A Note from Glenda Sanders

The media constantly tells us that it's a jungle out there for singles. Men can't commit, women don't want to be forced into traditional roles and fidelity is dead.

Yet, the truth is that romance—the process of falling in love—is timeless. The magic, the thrill, the enchantment are the same for contemporary women in sweatbands as they were for mythical princesses in coronets. So, while we can't all go to the ball wearing glass slippers, we can be part of a romantic fairy tale that is uniquely ours.

For me, the romantic tale began when I was at college, working as a sports reporter on a college paper, and met the captain of the rifle team. I went with him to a match. Afterward, his teammates put a Just Married banner on his car to embarrass him. Instead of making a scene that would embarrass him, I cuddled up next to him and gave him a kiss on the cheek.

Less than a year later, those same buddies were putting a real Just Married banner on the same car. And in a few months, we will have lived together for a quarter of a century—quite happily, thank you!

Books by Glenda Sanders

HARLEQUIN TEMPTATION
356–A HUMAN TOUCH
383–BABY CAKES
402–HAUNTING SECRETS

WIN-A-FORTUNE

OFFICIAL RULES • MILLION DOLLAR SWEEPSTAKES
NO PURCHASE OR OBLIGATION NECESSARY TO ENTER

To enter, follow the directions published. **ALTERNATE MEANS OF ENTRY:** Hand-print your name and address on a 3″×5″ card and mail to either: Harlequin Win-A-Fortune, 3010 Walden Ave., P.O. Box 1867, Buffalo, NY 14269-1867, or Harlequin Win A Fortune, P.O. Box 609, Fort Erie, Ontario L2A 5X3, and we will assign your Sweepstakes numbers (Limit: one entry per envelope). For eligibility, entries must be received no later than March 31, 1994 and be sent via 1st-class mail. No liability is assumed for printing errors or lost, late or misdirected entries.

To determine winners, the sweepstakes numbers on submitted entries will be compared against a list of randomly preselected prizewinning numbers. In the event all prizes are not claimed via the return of prizewinning numbers, random drawings will be held from among all other entries received to award unclaimed prizes.

Prizewinners will be determined no later than May 30, 1994. Selection of winning numbers and random drawings are under the supervision of D.L. Blair, Inc., an independent judging organization whose decisions are final. One prize to a family or organization. No substitution will be made for any prize, except as offered. Taxes and duties on all prizes are the sole responsibility of winners. Winners will be notified by mail. Chances of winning are determined by the number of entries distributed and received.

Sweepstakes open to persons 18 years of age or older, except employees and immediate family members of Torstar Corporation, D.L. Blair, Inc., their affiliates, subsidiaries and all other agencies, entities and persons connected with the use, marketing or conduct of this Sweepstakes. All applicable laws and regulations apply. Sweepstakes offer void wherever prohibited by law. Any litigation within the province of Quebec respecting the conduct and awarding of a prize in this Sweepstakes must be submitted to the Régies des Loteries et Courses du Quebec. In order to win a prize, residents of Canada will be required to correctly answer a time-limited arithmetical skill-testing question. Values of all prizes are in U.S. currency.

Winners of major prizes will be obligated to sign and return an affidavit of eligibility and release of liability within 30 days of notification. In the event of non-compliance within this time period, prize may be awarded to an alternate winner. Any prize or prize notification returned as undeliverable will result in the awarding of the prize to an alternate winner. By acceptance of their prize, winners consent to use of their names, photographs or other likenesses for purposes of advertising, trade and promotion on behalf of Torstar Corporation without further compensation, unless prohibited by law.

This Sweepstakes is presented by Torstar Corporation, its subsidiaries and affiliates in conjunction with book, merchandise and/or product offerings. Prizes are as follows: Grand Prize—$1,000,000 (payable at $33,333.33 a year for 30 years). First through Sixth Prizes may be presented in different creative executions, each with the following approximate values: First Prize—$35,000; Second Prize—$10,000; 2 Third Prizes—$5,000 each; 5 Fourth Prizes—$1,000 each; 10 Fifth Prizes—$250 each; 1,000 Sixth Prizes—$100 each. Prizewinners will have the opportunity of selecting any prize offered for that level. A travel-prize option if offered and selected by winner, must be completed within 12 months of selection and is subject to hotel and flight accommodations availability. Torstar Corporation may present this sweepstakes utilizing names other than Million Dollar Sweepstakes. For a current list of all prize options offered within prize levels and all names the Sweepstakes may utilize, send a self-addressed stamped envelope (WA residents need not affix return postage) to: Million Dollar Sweepstakes Prize Options/Names, P.O. Box 7410, Blair, NE 68009.

For a list of prizewinners (available after July 31, 1994) send a separate, stamped self-addressed envelope to: Million Dollar Sweepstakes Winners, P.O. Box 4728, Blair NE 68009.

SWP-H493

Where do you find hot Texas nights, smooth Texas charm and dangerously sexy cowboys?

AMARILLO BY MORNING

Show time—Texas style!

Everybody loves a cowboy, and Cal McKinney is one of the best. So when designer Serena Davis approaches this handsome rodeo star, the last thing Cal expects is a business proposition!

CRYSTAL CREEK reverberates with the exciting rhythm of Texas. Each story features the rugged individuals who live and love in the Lone Star State. And each one ends with the same invitation...

Y'ALL COME BACK...REAL SOON!

Don't miss *AMARILLO BY MORNING* by Bethany Campbell. Available in May wherever Harlequin books are sold.

---

*O*nce upon a time...

THERE WAS A FABULOUS
PROOF-OF-PURCHASE OFFER
AVAILABLE FROM

As you enjoy your Harlequin Temptation LOVERS & LEGENDS
stories each and every month during 1993, you can collect four
proofs of purchase to redeem a lovely opal pendant! The classic
look of opals is always in style, and this necklace is a perfect
complement to any outfit!

One proof of purchase can be found in the back pages of each
LOVERS & LEGENDS title...one every month during 1993!

LIVE THE FANTASY...

To receive your gift, mail this certificate, along with four (4) proof-of-purchase coupons from
any Harlequin Temptation LOVERS & LEGENDS title plus $2.50 for postage and handling (check
or money order—do not send cash), payable to Harlequin Books, to: **In the U.S.**: LOVERS &
LEGENDS, P.O. Box 9057, Buffalo, NY 14269-9057; **In Canada**: LOVERS & LEGENDS, P.O.
Box 622, Fort Erie, Ontario L2A 5X3.
Requests must be received by January 31, 1994.
Allow 4-6 weeks after receipt of order for delivery.

NAME: _____

ADDRESS: _____

_____

CITY: _____

STATE/PROVINCE: _____

ZIP/POSTAL CODE: _____

ONE PROOF OF PURCHASE   084 KAO LLPOPR